The Shadow Girl

Mary Sheldon, the daughter of
Sidney Sheldon and a novelist in her own
right, grew up in Los Angeles and New
York City. She attended St Clare's Hall,
Oxford before going to Yale and Wel-
lesley. She lives in Los Angeles. *The
Shadow Girl* is her third novel.

MARY SHELDON

The Shadow Girl

Fontana Paperbacks

British Library Cataloguing in Publication Data

Sheldon, Mary
    The shadow girl.
    I. Title
    813'.54 [F]   PS3569.H39266

    ISBN 0-00-617384-5

First published by Fontana Paperbacks 1987

Made and printed in Great Britain by
William Collins & Sons Co. Ltd., Glasgow

For my daughter, Elizabeth Rowane –

'O wonderful, wonderful and most wonderful wonderful! And yet again, wonderful . . .'

I would like to thank Collins Publishers, and in particular Laura Longrigg, whose efforts on this book have been nearly as tireless as my own!

I would also like to thank:
Papa,
The living spirit of my Mama,
Barry Dastin,
Dorris Halsey,
and the Mad Monk of Manhattan Beach, Christopher Stone.

PROLOGUE

They were seven years old, on a day of high blue wind. They had heard the mournful music of the ice-cream man in the park, and were running as fast as they could towards him.

'Two vanilla ice creams. As usual,' he said when he saw them. Then he said something he had never said before. 'One for the girl and one for her shadow.'

And he switched on his music again, and started up his van.

'Wait a minute,' Terry said. 'Which one's the girl and which one's the shadow?'

The man only laughed.

Julie started running as hard as she could, into the wind. 'I'm the girl!' she shrieked. 'And you're only the shadow!'

Terry was abreast of her in a moment. '*I'm* the girl! And *you're* the shadow!'

They ran and ran into the hot blue day.

CHAPTER ONE

The Plaza Hotel was lovely on that afternoon in early fall. It nestled like a baby, supported by a blanket of sky. The huge flags flew over the entrance, while in the rooms small lamps began to glow like night-lights.

The passers-by took no notice. Outside on 59th Street, stooping executives carried heavy briefcases and wished they felt energetic enough to walk home. Salesladies with burning bunions at Bergdorf Goodman's waited for the last shoppers to leave. Secretaries dizzy with five o'clock freedom scowled at the huge line of people also waiting for the cross-town bus. Limousines waited like fat lap dogs. Puffing taxis dashed. But inside the Plaza Hotel, the Palm Court was alive with the clatter of afternoon tea, and there was music and rose and cream and green and gold.

Theresa Spenser came down in the brass elevator and walked into the lobby. She was elegantly dressed in a suit of pale grey wool, but even the ruffled silk collar around her neck did not ease the air of astrigency she carried about with her. She held her Hermes handbag firmly under her arm as if she was expecting to be mugged. She was an attractive woman, with her firm, long face, her thick dark hair slightly touched with grey, and her graceful, ascetic body, but a look of preoccupation was superimposed over all her features, blurring their effect. It was her habitual expression.

She found herself facing a small bulletin board.

5.15. Grand Ballroom. Theresa Spenser. 'Mechanics of Mothering'.

Theresa drew in a small, sharp breath. Even after five years of giving lectures, it still afforded her a surprised start to see her name displayed on boards or printed on programmes. Not a thrill, especially, just a surprise.

She climbed up the stairs to the Grand Ballroom.

'Dear Mrs Spenser! How wonderful to see you!' Mrs Eagerman, the chairwoman, had espied her over the tea-urn, and swarmed over. She took Theresa's arm and questioned her with desperate seriousness as to how she had slept, whether the room was warm enough, whether the microphone was at the right height. A great weariness began to drag at Theresa. She had known too many Mrs Eager-mans, with the heavy gold chains circling their obviously surgeon-taut necks, their heavy scent of Chloe, heavy hairdos, heavy ankles. Then she felt annoyed at herself for her disgust. How dared she be so ungrateful? For as long as she could remember, hadn't this been her dream – to do something important and be recognized for it? Hadn't this been precisely what she'd fantasized about, all those years with Michael in that dreary Evanston apartment?

The meeting was called to order promptly at 5.15. Theresa walked upon the dais, and looked down at the rows of women seated on their stiff chairs. Mrs Eagerman lost no opportunity to hold forth.

'If I were to take the time to list all the innovations Theresa Spenser has introduced in the area of daycare,' she began, 'the rent on this room alone would bankrupt our Club. Why, just the other day, I was looking over the brochure of her pre-school centres, and I was startled by their resemblance to college catalogues; classes in Braille and sign language, photography, Israeli folk dance, computer technology. And every week, guest lecturers from museums, businesses and universities, speaking on everything from Grecian pottery to raising chickens to finger painting. But all this can hardly be news to you. Most of you here today have probably had the privilege of being involved with a Theresa Spenser daycare centre, and if not, why, her work must still be familiar to you from the stories written about her in *Time* and *Newsweek* and the *Journal of Higher Education* . . .'

Theresa tried to listen with appreciation to Mrs Eagerman's introduction, but the longer it went on, the more chilled she became. Why do I sound more and more like an obituary? she wondered.

'And now,' Mrs Eagerman finally wound up, 'it gives me the very greatest pleasure to introduce to you . . .'

When Theresa finished her speech, she was surprised to find how drained she was. She could not even remember several of the points she had discussed. That was eerie. The applause, as always, was spontaneous and enthusiastic.

At last it was all over, and she could sit down again. As she leaned back against her stiff chair, she felt that her silk blouse was wet through.

The meeting was adjourned. Mrs Eagerman, sleek with the consciousness of the speech's success, smiled a chicken-à-la-king smile and congratulated Theresa. There were offers of a glass of wine, a further chat, but Theresa explained about the terrible headache she had and asked to be excused. Afterwards, she was surprised she had said that. She did not usually lie.

She was glad to leave the Grand Ballroom. It was sane and cool in the hallway. She reached the large staircase to the lobby and peered down. She could hear the sounds of laughing shoppers, rushing footsteps on the rosy carpet, the sounds of the violins in the Palm Court. Theresa felt as she had when she was a little girl, watching through the banisters while her parents were having a party downstairs. Cheated. She had a sudden strange urge to join the party now.

Almost without thinking, Theresa went down the stairs and found herself facing the Palm Court. She gazed at it for a moment; the waiters dipping among the marble-topped tables, the palms in their pale porcelain urns, the large iced cakes being sliced with ornate silver knives, and she smiled. The Palm Court was just as she had remembered it. Exactly. On that day when she – when she and Julie had come there.

Theresa was to attend a formal dinner at eight, and she had intended to spend the time between reviewing data for the following day's meeting. But she was powerless. She was not going to go up to her room. She was going to have tea in the Palm Court. Just as she had done then – that time which seemed so long ago.

She waited behind the velvet rope for a table, unaware that she was the only lone woman there. Theresa had stopped worrying about things like that several years before. In only a moment she was led to a choice spot near the trio of musicians. The maitre d' had recognized the quality of her wool suit.

Theresa sat down. The room seemed warm. She took out her compact from her handbag and looked in a perfunctory way at her face. Yes, she looked faded; but then she always did. The compact was quickly returned.

The Palm Court was filled mainly with women, cheerful-looking, replete. One or two sulky girls in crumpled Dalton school uniforms squirmed with boredom as they had tea with their mothers. There were a few hope-to-be actresses dressed in gold lamé cocktail outfits with what seemed to be gold lamé hair, their long necks swivelling towards any newcomer. And there was one grandly dressed old man in a wheelchair who ate his crème caramel with careful, trembling bites, smiling at the music he could no longer hear.

Theresa looked around and was filled with a sense of depression. She remembered how wonderfully dressed and sophisticated all these tea-drinkers had seemed the last time she sat here. That was when she had wanted to be a fashion designer and she had furtively sketched every woman's outfit on the paper coaster beneath her Coca-Cola. Had they really all been so beautiful then, or was it simply because she had been fifteen years old?

The waiter came over. 'What can we get for you today, Madame?'

'Just some Earl Grey tea, please.'

'Why – Mrs Spenser!' Behind Theresa came a voice of thundering triumph. Turning around, she saw Mrs Eagerman pressing her way through the room, like a tidal wave capsizing the tiny tables. 'You look like you've recovered from your headache,' she was crying. 'How marvellous! I always say, there's nothing like a good cup of tea to work miracle cures.'

Theresa, ashamed of the lie she had told, said nothing.

'It must be Fate,' the chairwoman went on eagerly, reaching Theresa's table, 'our meeting again like this. I was just thinking over your simply marvellous speech, and there are so many little questions I'd love to ask you. Do let me buy you another cup of tea. Then we can really talk.' She sat down.

'I'm afraid there were several wee points I disagreed with in your speech,' Mrs Eagerman began archly. And for the next twenty-five minutes, she talked.

Finally Theresa looked down at her watch. 'Mrs Eagerman,' she said firmly, 'this is most interesting, but I'm afraid I really must – '

The chairwoman clapped a plump hand over her mouth. 'What have I been doing? Babbling on at you like this, when you must have a hundred things you want to do.'

Theresa said nothing.

'Do you know New York well?' Mrs Eagerman asked.

'Not really. Actually I've only been here once before – when I was fifteen. I didn't have a very good time.'

'How terrible. I hope this trip will be more meaningful.' Mrs Eagerman paused, then added with a gleam, 'Perhaps you might like me to show you around a few of the more – '

'Oh, that's very kind of you,' Theresa said hastily, 'but I'm afraid I'm going to be terribly busy with lectures and meetings. And I promised my son I'd search out the latest electronics gadget for him, whatever it may be.'

'Oh, yes; your son Christopher,' the chairwoman said

with warm interest. Theresa had written many an article about her son. 'How old is he now?'

'Nearly sixteen.'

'And he's back home in Illinois?'

A wave of longing for her son stung Theresa. 'Yes.'

'I bet he's giving his daddy a hard time!' Mrs Eagerman said knowingly.

Theresa froze. This was something she did not talk about, did not like talking about. 'No,' she said. 'Christopher is with the housekeeper. His father is out of the country.'

She thought that evasion would solve it.

'I see. And how long has he been out of the country?' Mrs Eagerman pursued.

'A year or two.'

'You're not sure when he left?' The chairwoman's eyes were avid.

'No. We were no longer married.'

Theresa looked away from the expression of indecent interest that spread over Mrs Eagerman's squashed features. It was always that way when people found out that Theresa Spenser, family expert, was divorced.

At that moment, the trio of musicians began to play the 'Tennessee Waltz'.

Theresa drew in her breath sharply. The Tennessee Waltz. She felt light-headed – as if she were going to start hyperventilating. Around her the Palm Court, the smiling faces began to fizzle and shrink to nothing. Once again she was five years old. She was driving down Santa Monica Boulevard with her mother in the blue Imperial convertible, and Patti Page was singing on the radio.

I was dancing with my darlin' to the Tennesse Waltz,
When an old friend I happened to see.
Introduced him to my loved one, and while they were waltzing
My friend stole my sweetheart from me.

And little Terry was clamping her hands over her ears to shut out that betrayal.

'Turn it off, Mama!'

But her mother did not believe in giving in to fear. She said loudly, so that Terry could hear her even through her swaddled ears, 'Don't be silly, Terry. It's only a song. It isn't real.'

But it had always been real to Theresa.

She blinked. How absolutely idiotically she was behaving. Theresa forced herself to return to the present, and drew the Palm Court into focus again. She looked around. She studied the quilted backs of the chairs, the pattern of the silver. She watched the dwindling line of waiting tea-drinkers. And then she saw a woman walking towards her table.

The woman was very small. She was dressed in a dress of printed silk, and the bones on her shoulders stuck out like the beating wings of little birds. But it was her hair – her hair like a thick white dandelion flying out from the sides of her thin face. Theresa stared. Oh God. Oh God. Nobody else could have that hair.

Abruptly, Theresa rose. Her teacup jangled against its saucer as she jarred the table. 'I'm sorry,' she said to Mrs Eagerman. 'I'm sorry. I must go.'

Clutching her suit jacket and handbag, she walked swiftly from the room. As she reached the entrance, the musical instruments slowed and then stopped. The 'Tennessee Waltz' was over.

It was a chilly September morning in Brentwood, California. An eerie and unfamiliar fog rode grimly on the top of the autumn flower gardens, the postman's cap, the swimming pools. All the houses that had been so gay in the summer looked chastened and afraid, like the grasshopper in the fable who forgot to think of winter.

In a small private school, so expensive that her parents could not really afford to send her there, a little girl was sitting at her desk. It was the first day of first grade, and Terry Garvey thought she was going to die. She had looked forward for so long to finally starting school, to finally being a grown-up; and now that the day was here, she had never felt as babyish in her life.

Terry was not a pretty child. Although her skin was wonderfully fair and her features so delicate they could have been blown from Venetian glass, the thick glasses she wore, the bluntly cut hair, and her nervous peering abolished any adorable little girlishness. Miss Summers, watching Terry from her teacher's desk at the front of the room, had already diagnosed her as a potential problem child. Antisocial tendencies, she thought – and definitely hyperactive.

Terry squirmed desperately at her desk, trying to get comfortable. Her mother had trimmed her bangs that morning, and spears of cut hair kept stinging her neck. And the collar of her new dress from J.C. Penney's felt like it was made out of a hairy Brillo pad.

None of the other children had arrived yet. It was very embarrassing, being alone in the room with Miss Summers like this. Terry very much wished she could think of something intriguing and intelligent to say, something that would make the teacher like her. She had already said, 'I can count to ten in Spanish,' 'My brother Timmy had an operation on his adenoids,' and 'Do you tease your hair to make it stick out like that?' but the teacher had not seemed at all impressed.

Sadly, Terry began to think of Sukie, her big rag doll with yellow yarn hair. Sukie was at home now, sitting on the windowseat in her bedroom, missing her so much – why, she might even be crying. Terry began to feel rather like crying herself. She wished the other children would come. She wondered what would happen if no one ever came, and she was locked in this room with Miss Summers forever. Her hands began to give off a smell of bacon, the way they always did when she was scared, and she worried that Miss Summers would notice the smell and think that Terry had been sneaking food to school in her pockets.

At last the classroom door opened and, one by one, the rest of the children arrived. The headmistress, squat Mrs Delaney, brought each one in, gripping them by the shoulders and introducing them.

Terry grew more and more anxious as child after child appeared. She could tell right away that she was going to hate them all. They looked so tough and so mean. Terry despaired. Was there time to make a dash for it? Out of the door and home? But Mrs Delaney was standing there. Was she really growing bigger every second? Terry slumped, mute and defeated, in her chair.

Amidst all this activity, Miss Summers had risen from her desk and come to life. She was taking coats and asking everyone their birthdays and what their daddies did. Terry could tell that Miss Summers liked all the other children more than she liked her.

Then the door opened one final time.

'Class, this is Julie Adams.'

Terry sat up and gulped back a little sound of wonder. Julie Adams was the most beautiful girl she had ever seen. She was like some sort of precious doll. She had wide, frightened grey eyes and incredible curly hair that stuck out from her head like a sparkler on the Fourth of July. It was so pale that it glowed, and it was held in place by a green velvet ribbon. And Julie was so tiny she looked almost unreal. She wore a checked pinafore with wee ruffled pockets, and her hands clutched at a minute black patent leather handbag. Terry couldn't believe it. She couldn't believe that anything so adorable could have just entered her life.

'Hello, Julie,' Miss Summers said.

The little girl curtsied gravely, and Terry fell utterly and instantly in love.

All morning long, Terry gazed at Julie Adams. She examined every feature of the little girl's face, noticed the tiny heart-shaped locket around her neck, saw how Julie knew all the words to 'I Pledge Allegiance', and almost laughed aloud at her delight in the pet gerbil.

Suppose she were in a train crash, Terry began to day-dream. What would I do? I would leap through the burning cars and pull her out to safety. Or, if all the children in the class turned on Julie and tied her to the jungle gym, I'd throw the football at them until they went away.

'Well, Theresa?' Miss Summers was saying tartly. 'This is the third time I've asked you if you know how to read. Dear me, girls, Theresa doesn't seem to have been paying attention at all!'

The whole class laughed. Terry stared down at her desktop, miserable and furious. She could not bear to lift her eyes and see if Julie Adams was laughing, too.

At last the morning's captivity was over, and the bell rang for lunchtime. The children jumped up from their desks and ran, hollering with relief, outside.

The morning fog had gone now, and the playground looked dreamy and green. Terry got out her paper lunch-bag and looked around for Julie Adams. Finally she saw her coming out of the door, hauling the strangest metal lunchbox Terry had ever seen. It looked like something a construction worker might carry. It was so huge and ungainly that it threatened to split Julie's frail arms in pieces. Seeing it, one of the big boys in the class began to snicker. His friends joined him. And soon everyone on the

18

playground had gathered in a circle around Julie, pointing, laughing, whispering.

Terry was desperate with rage. She longed to save Julie from this humiliation, but it wasn't as easy to be a heroine in real life as it had been in her fantasies. Then suddenly she thought of a way. She pushed herself roughly through the crowd of jeering children and stood in front of Julie, panting.

'For your information,' she told the ring of children angrily, 'this happens to be my lunchbox, not hers. She's just carrying it for me because she's my best friend. If you want to pick on me, go ahead – but I ought to tell you – my big brother Timmy has taught me karate.'

The children muttered uneasily at this information, and soon the circle broke up. Finally Terry and Julie were left alone.

'*Will* you be my best friend?' Terry asked.

Gravely Julie considered her. 'All right,' she said at last.

And, ever so gently, Terry lifted the heavy lunchbox from her best friend's arm.

'I've never seen a childhood friendship like it before,' Miss Summers complained to the headmistress. 'It's so intense it's almost spooky.'

'It'll cool off,' Mrs Delaney said.

'I'm not so sure,' the teacher murmured.

'Has this girl hypnotized you?' Mrs Garvey would ask, when Terry came home month after month with tales of what Julie had worn that day, or what she had said. 'Stop acting like such a baby about her.' But Terry didn't care.

'Julie, can you come over to my house on Saturday?' one of the other girls would ask. 'We might be going on a picnic.'

'I'm sorry – I'll be at Terry's.'

'Do you go there every Saturday?'

'Every Saturday.'

'You're weird.'

But Julie didn't care.

Terry and Julie. They were all that mattered to each other.

It was a bright spring morning. The day seemed to leap with freshness. Everything was mixed motion – the swirling clouds, the wind-bent grass, the toss of the washing on the line. Terry felt like spinning and spinning and never stopping.

She came into the kitchen. Her mother was sitting hunched on a stool, cutting up chicken. Terry watched distastefully, and with a little fear, the way her mother's hands inexorably tore at the pale flesh. Her euphoria began to drain away.

'Where's Daddy?' she asked.

'In the garage,' her mother said, a little sharply. 'As usual.'

Terry went into the garage. For several moments she watched her father without his knowing she was there. It made her smile to see him. Even outwardly, he looked different from all the other daddies she knew. He looked like something from one of Terry's colouring books, with his bright red beard and cat-green eyes and plaid shirt. He never wore grey suits to work, he didn't join any clubs, he didn't carry a briefcase. 'That's what comes from dropping out of college,' he would explain with a laugh.

Dropping out of college seemed to have made her father very smart, Terry thought. He could do electrical wiring, he could build a swimming pool, he knew the names of all the constellations. He had lived in Alaska for two years, and he had a tattoo of a peacock on his arm. He even had a wooden leg, because his real one had got sick and had to be cut off. That wooden leg seemed to be bothering him now, for he grimaced as he stepped on it. Terry hated to see him make faces like that.

'Daddy!' she said, stepping into the garage.

He turned to her, smiling, his leg forgotten. 'I'm working on the train set. Want to watch?'

Terry shook her head. Ordinarily she loved watching her father adding to the enormous train set he had constructed on a plywood board – but this Saturday morning in March she had more serious matters to discuss.

'Julie's coming over today,' she announced.

'Yes?'

Her father did not seem surprised, since Julie came over every Saturday. Mrs Adams, Terry's mother often remarked bitterly, obviously did not believe in reciprocity.

Terry swung on the handle of the garage door. This was a difficult request to make.

'Could you maybe ask Mama to put on her back and white dress?' she asked quickly. 'You know – the pretty one.'

Her father smiled. 'Why? Is it a special occasion?'

'Not really,' Terry stammered. 'It's just that Julie's mother always looks so pretty, and I want Julie to think Mama is pretty, too.'

She did not see the smile leave her father's face, so she rushed recklessly on. 'And maybe you could clean up the front yard a little. Last time she was over, Julie fell on the stoop and got her dress dirty. And maybe you could tell Timmy not to tease her and not to be such a big slob at lunch.'

'Did Julie ask you to say these things?' Terry's father asked quietly.

'Oh, no!' Terry beamed. 'Julie says she loves it here. I guess she's about the best guest in the whole word!'

'Terry,' Mr Garvey said after a long pause, 'I want to tell you something. I don't think Julie is a very good friend for you to have.'

'What?' Terry was so shocked she could hardly get the word out.

21

Her father went on, slowly but firmly. 'I have the feeling that she – isn't quite what she seems to be. That she's not quite, well, real. And I don't like the way she seems to have cast a spell over you.'

'What are you talking about?' Terry glared.

'Well, for one thing, before Julie Adams came along, I don't think you would have cared what dress your Mama wore.'

Terry was panting with fury. 'Julie's the nicest and the smartest and the prettiest girl in the world!'

'She can't be,' her father said, trying to smile. 'You are.'

Terry was aghast. She had never known her father to lie before. 'I'm not,' she cried. 'I'm ugly and I'm bad and I'm dumb.'

Mr Garvey put down the piece of track he had been working on. When he looked at Terry, she saw that he was very, very angry.

'Never say that again,' he told her in a low voice so filled with emotion that she was frightened. 'You're beautiful. You're smart and what's more, you're honest. You can be anything you want to be.'

'I don't want to be anything.' Terry told him in a muffled voice, 'unless you say that Julie Adams is the most wonderful girl in the world.'

But her father would not say that.

'Then I guess I won't be anything,' Terry said.

'I guess you won't,' he answered.

It was the middle of the night and Julie was asleep. The maid came in and softly awakened her.

'Your mother wants you, dear.'

Anxiously, Julie stumbled to her mother's room. Mrs Adams was lying in bed, sobbing.

'It's another headache, darling,' she gasped. 'I've taken three pills but they haven't helped at all. You're the only one who can make it go away.'

Julie climbed up onto the big bed. Pressing her hands to her mother's hot forehead, she began to massage it. Then she sang her a little song that she had learned at school, and kept murmuring that soon the headache would be all gone, all gone. She was so pleased when at last her mother's eyes closed, so proud when the tense shoulders relaxed at last. Sighing with joy, Julie went back to bed.

One Saturday morning in August, Terry woke early out of sheer excitement. Today was one of those rare miracle days – she had actually been invited to spend the morning at Julie's! She lay in bed and thought all about it, hating to get up and crease the perfection of her happy anticipation.

Julie's house, at the top of Cherokee Road, was enormous and romantic and a little bewildering. There were steep servants' staircases that hadn't been used for years, a salon filled with mirrored furniture, and a room where, if you pressed a certain magic button over the bar stool, a screen would come down and you could watch a movie. Terry had never actually watched a movie there – no one had in a long time – but Julie said they used to run them every Sunday afternoon and evening, with a buffet dinner in between. They called it their film festival. But that was when her actress mother and producer father were still married.

The house was always very dark, which bothered Terry. But in a way that made it all the nicer to come upstairs to Julie's room. Julie's room looked down on to the enormous swimming pool, and little spatters and sparkles of sunlight were reflected in at the windows, making the whole room look like the Little Mermaid's palace at the bottom of the sea. Everything in this bower, the snowy bed canopy, the glazed furniture, the pink and white flowered wallpaper, was perfect for Julie. And Julie had a wallful of toys that more than rivalled those at F.A.O. Schwartz; books with gold on the leather bindings, stuffed animals taller than she was, and a glass case of antique dolls, complete with tiny parasols and lace bonnets. Julie's mother preferred that she did not open the glass case too often, but it was magic just to look inside.

Over Julie's bed was a big oil painting of her mother sitting on a sofa. It was such a beautiful painting that Terry got a tender, sore feeling in her throat every time she looked at it. A long time ago, Julie told Terry, her mother had been a big star in the movies, and all through the house there were portraits of her, done by loyal fans – people who didn't forget, she explained.

Terry thought Mrs Adams should still be a big star. There was nobody prettier than Julie's mother, with her round blue eyes that looked like they were made of glass, the fluffy auburn hair standing around her head, the smile that never quite interrupted the stillness of her face, and her sweet, low-pitched drawl.

She wasn't like any mother Terry had ever seen. She never went bowling or talked about what she had bought at the department store sale, and she never never wore pixie bands in her hair. She lay in bed a lot, smoking and reading books with beautiful women on the covers, and she wore nightgowns that were so lacy and stylish she could have gone to a party in them. And whenever she spoke to Julie, her voice was so soft and loving that it sounded like a warm cat's purr. Terry had never dreamed a mother could sound like that. Just thinking about it, she began to roll over and over in delight amongst the bedclothes. She loved Julie's mother! She loved Julie's house! She loved Julie!

The two girls were going to a matinée after lunch that day, so Terry had to look her best. Usually her mother bought her clothes that could be slipped into easily – Mrs Garvey did not have time to hook hooks or buttons – but for this occasion, Terry had a new brown skirt and pink blouse with eleven buttons up the back.

Terry hated the feel of her mother's hands climbing up

her spine, and she twitched irritably. Then abruptly she stopped, as she felt those hands stiffen. If pushed too far, Mrs Garvey had a tendency to slap – and the last thing Terry wanted was to appear at Julie's house with a big mark on her face.

At last the buttoning was finished, but still Mrs Garvey wouldn't let her go. She held her by the arm and started asking questions Terry found very strange.

'Terry, is Julie's mother always home when you go over to their house? She's never left you alone, has she?'

'Oh, no,' Terry answered brightly.

'Are there ever any men who come over to visit?'

'No.'

'Do you ever see Mrs Adams acting strangely – as if she can't walk straight?'

'No.'

Mrs Garvey coughed delicately. 'Do you like Julie's mother, Terry? Or do you think there's something a little unusual about her, maybe?'

Terry thought of beautiful Mrs Adams lying in bed with a tray of champagne glasses on her silk sheets, and laughing with all the nice men who were always coming by.

'No,' she lied dreamily. 'She's just like all the other mothers. Except she's more beautiful. She's the most beautiful mother I ever saw.'

Mrs Garvey dropped her hands with a hurt gasp, and Terry spun happily away – free.

Julie and her mother were in bed together, watching one of Mrs Adams' movies on the late show. Julie was drinking her fourth Coke, Mrs Adams her fourth martini.

'The critics panned this from here to Alaska,' her mother told her in a strange blurred voice. 'That was because the Bastard released it at the wrong time.'

The Bastard was Julie's father. It was the only name her mother ever called him by – at least, when she had

had more than two martinis.

'How did you meet him?' Julie asked softly. She had always wanted to know.

Her mother paused. 'I was a schoolgirl,' she said in a low voice. 'He was shooting a picture, near my home town in Colorado. I came with all my friends to see the shooting. He spotted me and asked if I'd like to be in the crowd scene. I said yes.' She pressed her hand against her mouth, and Julie could barely hear her next words. 'As it turned out, in the final cut he never used me. But he used me in every other way he could think of.'

Julie loved going to her grandmother's house for tea. It was so safe and peaceful there, and the blue Wedgwood china made her happy because it was so beautiful.

'Granny,' Julie asked suddenly, 'did Daddy like me?'

'Of course he did,' her grandmother said readily. 'I remember when he came to the hospital to see you. He was positively dancing.'

'And did he – like Mummy?' Julie breathed.

'I have never seen a man so in love with a woman in my life,' her grandmother said in a strange voice.

On a sweet fresh Easter morning, Julie and her mother were emerging hand in hand from the little church on Wilshire Boulevard where they had attended the morning service. Terry, invited for the day, walked shyly a few steps behind, watching the two of them a little wistfully. Julie's tiny arm was strained high to meet her mother's, and they pressed fingers closely. Mother and daughter were dressed alike, in white linen A-line dresses and white gloves. Mrs Adams carried a large white handbag and Julie wore a little eyelet bonnet so that the sun wouldn't scold her eyes.

'Oh, Mummy,' she pleaded, 'couldn't we go to the Park for a little while?'

Her mother smiled down tenderly. 'That's where we're headed.'

Terry was not surprised. Julie and her mother seemed to have the same thoughts, always.

Beverly Hills Park was deeply green that day, without the pastel innocence of the rest of the morning. There was a shifting, primitive force about it that made Julie squirm excitedly. Terry had never seen her like that before. Julie began to run about in mindless swooping circles, but her mother stopped her gently.

'Don't do that,' she said. 'It's not pretty. Let's see my little girl try to catch a butterfly instead.'

She took a small camera from her bag and focused it.

Terry watched, enchanted, as, holding up her skirts like a ballerina, Julie made many dainty rushes upon tiptoe, her hands cupping hundreds of imaginary butterflies.

'That's my princess,' Mrs Adams breathed, taking picture after picture. 'And now let's see Julie talking to a fairy.'

Julie sat down carefully on a stone bench so as not to soil her skirt, and earnestly gazed down at her palm as if a cross-legged elf were sitting upon it.

'How are you, fairy?' she inquired gently. 'I am very well, thank you.'

The camera clicked again and again. But never once was it turned on Terry, who understood perfectly.

'I think this is the sort of park the Easter Bunny might live in,' Mrs Adams said at last. 'Don't you think so, Julie?'

Julie bit back a sigh and shook her head imperceptibly. Terry looked at her sympathetically. She knew what was wrong. Julie had confessed that all morning long she had looked for the Easter Bunny and his offerings – by her bed, next to her plate at breakfast, in her coat pockets, all at her mother's urging. But he simply hadn't come.

Mrs Adams walked behind a shady tree for a moment, explaining that she had to change some film. When she came out again, the camera was in her bag.

'I think I'll sit on this bench and rest a moment,' she said. 'You two go play for a while. Why don't you go underneath the tree where I was? It's nice and cool there.'

Julie and Terry went off to the tree. They were just starting a game of 'Hide and Seek' when Julie gave a sudden gasp. There, on the mossy roots beneath an elm, was a little silver filigree basket. Inside, it was filled with chocolate eggs and wild flowers, and on top was a tiny gold bracelet inscribed, 'To Julie – the best little girl in the world – from the Easter Bunny with love.'

Julie was trembling so hard she could not get the bracelet on her wrist, and Terry had to do it for her. Julie staggered back to her mother on the bench, the basket in her hands. Her face blazed with joy. 'He came, Mummy,' she whispered.

Mrs Adams drew Julie into a feverish embrace. Neither she nor Julie seemed aware that Terry was there. 'You're Mummy's little angel,' she said passionately. 'I love you so. Promise me – promise me you'll never get a day older than you are right now.'

Gravely, Julie promised.

It was a rainy Saturday and Terry and Julie were in the breakfast room of Julie's house. They were lying on the floor, each painting a picture of a pond with the new set of French watercolours Julie's mother had given her for her eighth birthday. Terry was now adding dainty water lilies to her drawing, and Julie, struggling to remember what a duck looked like, watched with uneasy envy as the white blooms quickened under Terry's expert fingers.

'Boy, I sure wish my mother would buy me paints like this,' sighed Terry. 'But all I get are supermarket crayons.'

Julie bit her lip and looked from one painting to the other. The comparison was ludicrous. Terry's was a masterpiece, and her own looked like it could have been done by the cat. And yet she was the one who had the expensive paints. It seemed so awfully wrong and unfair. But then, wasn't it that way in just about everything? she asked herself mournfully. Terry's the one who can do spread eagles, but I'm the one who's got the imported roller skates. Terry's the one who can do a handstand, but I'm the one with the gymnastics mat. She's better at everything – everything, Julie thought. The only thing I am is richer.

'Maybe I'll be an artist when I grow up,' Terry said dreamily. 'That would be fun.'

Julie hated it when Terry went on like this, about what she was going to be when she grew up. Every week there was some new dream. And Julie didn't have even one.

'Hey,' Terry said suddenly, glancing over at her friend's painting. 'That's all wrong. Ducks don't have paws – they have webbed feet – like this.' She grabbed the brush out of Julie's hand and began re-painting vigorously.

'Leave it alone!' Julie stormed, hanging on to the other end of the paper. 'I meant it to look like that!'

'Sorry,' Terry said quickly, and went back to her own painting. But in a moment she could see the tears of humiliation rising in Julie's eyes. 'Hey, Julie,' she said hastily, 'I've got a great idea. You know what we should do with our pictures? Antique them.'

Julie blinked. 'What?'

'Give them the old-fashioned look. It's really easy. I'll show you.'

It *was* easy, Julie thought, comforted. You just put a little dark-brown paint on the bristles of your brushes, bend them back as far as they could go, and let them fly. Soon, authentic-looking flyspecks began to appear all over the two paintings.

Julie forgot her depression in the excitement of the artistic experiment. 'I'm going to give my picture to Mummy when it's done,' she said dreamily, as she worked.

Terry felt a little jealous. Even if the duck wasn't very wonderful, it would have been nice if Julie had given it to her. 'Well, *I'm* putting my painting in my bedroom,' she said a little sourly. 'My mother doesn't like my stuff cluttering up the house.'

Julie didn't say anything, but Terry could tell she felt sorry for her, having a mother like that. 'Doesn't your mother ever tell you you're making a mess?' she asked aggressively, seeing Julie's expression.

'No,' Julie said in a low voice.

'Doesn't she *ever* get mad at you?' Terry demanded, exasperated.

'Oh, no,' Julie answered, and a strange look came into the grey eyes. 'I'm Mummy's one and only.'

And this time Terry felt a double blast of jealousy. Not only did Julie love her mother more than she loved Terry, but Julie's mother loved Julie more than Terry's mother loved *her* . . .

She scowled and gave an especially vigorous shake to the paintbrush. 'There,' she said, holding up her painting. 'That's done.'

'They look so pretty, so pretty,' Julie smiled. 'Mummy will be so happy.' And then she looked up and screamed.

Within a radius of six feet, every inch of the wallpaper was completely covered in tiny brown paint spots.

Julie leapt up, not noticing that she was stepping on her duck painting, crushing it into the rug. She began to scrub desperately at the wallpaper with her small white fists, smearing the paint, smearing the paper, smearing her hands, making it worse.

'We've got to get it off!' she gibbered. 'We've got to!' She backed off from the wall, panting and pale. 'She'll kill me! She'll kill me!'

And from the terror in her friend's eyes, Terry suddenly realized how afraid of her mother Julie really was.

The relief of discovering that the paint came off with soap and water was nearly unbearable. Julie went into the bathroom and vomited wretchedly.

*

It was Halloween, and an appropriately ghostly dusk was descending. Terry stood before the large mirror in her parents' bedroom and looked at herself dourly. She felt like a fool in her Batman costume. The legs were too short, and the too-big mask had had to be anchored in the back by a row of plastic pink barrettes. Terry didn't even like Batman, but that costume had been on sale in the department store, and her mother had been only too delighted to buy it.

Terry moved from side to side, making her plastic bat ears rustle behind her. She sighed. She had seen a television show the night before on Halloween safety. If I hit a Jack O'Lantern candle, she thought gloomily, the whole costume'll go up in flames and there won't be anything left of me but ashes. If I eat an unwrapped sweet, I'll probably have to have my stomach pumped. If I play a trick on anyone who doesn't give me a treat, I'll be arrested for juvenile delinquency.

Her ten-year-old brother Timmy passed along the hallway, singing two lines of a popular song. He sang them over and over – wrongly, Terry noted with secret satisfaction. Seeing her, Timmy stopped and came into the room. He looked critically at the costume.

'You look pretty dumb,' he said. There was some sympathy in his voice, so Terry nodded.

'I know.'

Timmy sat down on the lumpy king-size bed. 'Julie coming over?'

'Uh huh.' Terry sounded a little subdued. 'We're going trick-or-treating in her limousine. She's going as Dorothy from 'The Wizard of Oz'. Her mother paid someone to make her dress. She's even getting a little toy Toto.'

Timmy looked at his sister. 'Honestly,' he said, shaking his head. 'I don't know why that girl wastes her time on you.'

Terry's mouth sagged. She grew very red. She began to hit Timmy with her black-gloved fists, and butt him with her cowled head. He was laughing, holding her off. She was screaming, 'I hate you! I hate you!'

One Monday Terry was absent from school. Julie didn't like it when Terry was away – it made her feel so terribly alone. For apart from Terry, she had no friends.

She walked out to the playing field at recess. Nancy Spector, one of the sixth graders, had broken her arm that weekend. A group of girls was around her, felt pens in their hands, signing warm wishes on the cast.

Nancy was a kind girl. She spotted Julie in the shadows and called out cheerfully, 'Come on, Julie. You sign, too.'

Julie only gazed at the white-coated arm in horror. Louder and louder warned her mother's voice in her head: 'Don't touch dirty water! You'll get polio. Don't touch the dog! You'll get rabies. Don't touch . . . For God's sake, don't touch!'

'I can't touch!' Julie wanted to scream. If I do, I'll get a broken arm, too! But fear closed her throat, and she could only stand, unable to move.

'Look, she's scared!' one of the big boys shouted.

'Maybe she can't walk over!' another cried. 'Maybe she can't do anything without Terry Garvey.'

'Let's help her, then.'

And the crowd of children around Nancy moved towards Julie. She fought them off with desperate screams, but at last they overpowered her, dragged her over, and forced her to touch the white cast.

When Julie woke from her faint, she was in the nurse's office. She was very glad when Terry returned to school the next day.

The Garveys had a tradition – on the last evening of summer vacation they went for a sunset picnic on the beach. Terry, though she didn't admit it, always enjoyed these outings. And this year, she was in an especially good mood. She had gone to the beauty shop that afternoon, and her mother had paid for her to have her hair styled a daring new way. It was the 'flip' style worn by the heroine in the latest Elvis Presley movie. Terry thought she looked just like her. Maybe someone will come up to me and ask for my autograph, she thought dreamily.

'Terry! Get away from that mirror and hurry up!' her mother called. Terry was the last one in the car, and as she ran to it, she looked with affection at the family grouped inside. They weren't all bad, she thought grudgingly. Even Timmy looked almost like a normal human being today.

The weather at the beach was wonderful, and Terry and her mother set out the hamper. It occurred to Terry as she unpacked that her mother had gone to great trouble over it, devilling eggs, making brownies, even baking a trifle. Maybe I should have offered to help, she thought suddenly.

When the picnic was over, the sun was just setting. Terry sat shivering on the wind-whipped blanket and watched the sky. It had never seemed so beautiful; she had never felt so close to understanding – everything – when suddenly from behind her, there was a terrible jarring noise. It was her parents and Timmy, singing, 'On top of spaghetti, all covered with cheese.'

Terry cringed. Had they no soul at all? Were they deliberately trying to spoil all this beauty? She turned and looked at her family. They were all strangers to her.

Terry felt a great shock of aloneness and disappointment, I am not like these people, she thought slowly. We do not belong together, and we never will. I want to belong in Julie's world. I want to soar! I want to soar!

She took off from the blanket and began to run against the wind into the sunset. Running, running; the wind, the red, the sea, beckoning. Till suddenly an agonizing stinging in her foot brought her down onto the sand with a cry.

Her mother was over in a moment. 'Jellyfish sting,' she said briskly. 'I'll put some neosporin on it right away. I brought some along, just in case.'

'Thank you, Mama,' Terry whispered.

Julie was spending the night. She and Terry were lying together in Terry's big oak bed.

'Am I the best friend you ever had, Julie?' Terry whispered.

The confidence with which she asked the question had a strange effect on Julie. 'No.' she said.

She could not believe it once the words were out; could not understand why she had said such a thing. She could see Terry's shocked silhouette raised on one elbow.

'What?'

'I had another best friend,' Julie went on coolly. 'When we lived in New York.'

'I didn't know you ever lived in New York,' Terry said in bewilderment.

'Well, you don't know everything about me, do you?' Julie answered. 'Her name was Julie, just like mine, and we spent every day together. I told her everything. She was an orphan and she was almost adopted as my sister, except we had to go back to California.'

Terry lay back in bed, too stunned to speak. Half an hour later, when Julie was sure she was asleep, she leaned over and whispered, 'You're the best friend I ever had, Terry.' ·

Julie had honestly meant to study for the geography test. But 'The Red Shoes' had been on television the night before, and although she kept promising herself after every commercial that she would leave, she stayed until Moira Shearer jumped from the parapet; and then she was so depressed that she had to go straight to bed.

There were only fifteen minutes left in the test period, and Julie had only been able to answer two questions. Her head hung down. She felt very sick. Next to her was Terry, confidently racing through the exam, filling in the blanks with a sure pencil. Julie watched her miserably. At that moment, Terry looked up and saw Julie's white face. Then, looking down, she saw Julie's blank paper.

With a little sigh, Terry finished her test and leaned back in her chair. So far back, in fact, that Julie's view of her paper was completely unobstructed. Julie's eyes widened. She began to tremble. She knew it was wrong; oh, her mother would kill her if she found out; but she couldn't help it. Seizing her pencil, she desperately began to copy Terry's answers.

The following day, the tests were returned.

'What did you get?' Terry asked.

'I got an A,' Julie faltered.

Terry gave her the tiniest of smiles. 'Why, so did I,' she said.

On Wednesday afternoons, when Mrs Adams used her chauffeur, Julie rode home on the school bus with Terry. Terry loved these rides. She and Julie could sing and play word games and talk alone for thirty-five uninterrupted minutes.

And then in March of the sixth grade, the company decided to expand the bus route. One afternoon the driver, Mr Phillips, turned into the driveway of a small, dilapidated school in Brentwood, and opened his doors to the children. It made Terry upset to see these new commuters – girls who didn't look nearly as prosperous and clean as the ones who went to her school – scrambling together in a bunch at the back of the bus. At least they won't come bothering us, she thought thankfully.

But one little girl got up from her seat, staggered the length of the moving bus, and sat down right next to Terry and Julie. She was a stout little girl, with spiky brown hair and a bright-red vinyl jacket. Disconcerted, Terry started singing in a loud voice.

But the girl broke right into the song. 'Hi. My name's

Jackie. You two go to Pratt? Is that your briefcase? You have to carry briefcases? Shit! Let me see.'

And two dirty hands reached over and snatched Terry's briefcase from her lap. Terry was shocked. She could only watch unhappily as the dirty fingers ran over it and discovered all the secret little snaps and hiding places. Then it was thrown back to her.

'Junk this. It's not so cool,' Jackie exclaimed. 'My Dad makes leather goods. He could tell you.'

Losing interest in Terry and her briefcase, she turned to Julie. 'How old are you? What's your name? You're kinda little for the sixth grade. How much do you weigh?'

Terry didn't want Julie answering this awful girl. She tried to strike up another song but found, to her surprise, that Julie wasn't singing along.

'Sixty pounds,' Julie said.

'Only sixty pounds? That's damn light!'

Julie beamed. She loved being the smallest and daintiest.

'You know, you ought to get off the bus with me one day,' Jackie went on excitedly. 'We'd have a really good time – there's a park near my house. I could show you some neat new games.'

Julie smiled her sweetest smile at the little girl. She loved learning new games to play.

Terry was sour with jealousy. And then, when Julie and Jackie started singing together – singing the same song Terry and Julie had been singing five minutes before – Terry could stand it no longer.

'Listen, you – you hot shot girl – just leave us alone!'

'Nobody tells me what to do,' Jackie said. 'Not my Dad, not anybody. I'll fight you if I have to, but here's where I'm sitting.'

'Oh, yes, Terry!' Julie was suddenly plucking Terry's sleeve. Her face was alight with excitement. 'Oh, do fight with her!'

'No,' Terry said.

'I'll think you're a coward if you don't,' Julie warned.

Terry had no choice.

The two combatants moved into a big empty seat near the back of the bus, and began to claw and tussle. Terry didn't know the first thing about fighting, but she tried to look mean. The two enemies tugged and scratched for several minutes. Mr Phillips, who hadn't been at all pleased to have his bus route expanded, cried cheerfully, 'Give it to her, Terry!' And Julie, vivid with pleasure at the whole drama being enacted in her honour, called out shrill encouragement from the sidelines.

By the time Mr Phillips reached Mapleton Drive, things weren't going too well for Terry.

Suddenly Julie pulled her over. 'Tell her she has blood on her shoes, and then jump her!' she commanded in a thrilled whisper.

And so Terry did. Her pounce was perfect – she was satisfied and a little alarmed when she heard Jackie's vinyl jacket rip under the arm.

'You win,' Jackie said.

The next morning, when Terry and Julie got to school, they found their teacher, the dean and the headmistress waiting for them. The girls were taken into the office and told to sit down. Terry couldn't imagine what had happened.

'I have just had a telephone call,' the dean said weightily. 'An hysterical call from the mother of a child who goes to the Fisher School. Apparently, Theresa, yesterday on the school bus you beat the little girl black and blue. The mother has not made up her mind whether she is going to make a complaint to the police. I am at a loss as to what to say. Your parents have been contacted, of course, and I will leave your punishment to them.'

Terry began to tremble all over. She felt the dean's look had frozen up her tongue forever. She hadn't meant to hurt Jackie – she hadn't intended to pounce on her so hard . . .

The headmistress turned to Julie, a special favourite of hers. 'I know that you weren't involved in any of this, Julie,' she said gently. 'but did you see what was going on?'

Terry looked pleadingly over at Julie and waited for her support.

'I was taking a nap,' Julie answered innocently.

Terry drew in her breath sharply. She had been betrayed. For a moment she felt like telling Mrs Delaney all about how Julie was the one who made her fight in the first place, but she couldn't. Julie was her best friend.

'Mummy, how was I born?' Julie snuggled up to Mrs Adams.

'I talked to God,' Mrs Adams said, 'and I asked him to send me a tiny blonde princess with grey eyes and a freckle right here.'

'Would you have loved me if God had made a mistake?' Julie went on anxiously. 'If I'd been a boy, or had black hair or was tall?'

'No,' her mother said.

The girls were eight years old. Julie was spending one cold winter day at Terry's house. They were watching out of the living-room window with great interest as the Giovannis next door pulled into the driveway in their car. Mr Giovanni got out first and helped his wife carry a small blue-blanketed bundle into the house.

'I knew it would be a boy,' Terry said smugly. 'Because of the way she was carrying.'

Julie looked at her with such perplexity that Terry was amused. 'Gosh, Julie, don't you know how babies are born?'

'Oh, sure I do,' Julie said airily.

'Then tell me,' she challenged.

Timmy, unbeknownst to them, was standing by the open door. 'I'll tell you, Julie,' he volunteered. And before Terry could stop him, he told.

'I'll kill him for this,' Terry complained hotly to her parents that night. 'Julie was almost sick when she heard!'

Her parents exchanged a queer little smile.

'Don't make such a fuss,' her father said. 'She had to learn about it some time.'

There was an area behind the lower-school building known as 'the Hill', and as long as Terry and Julie had gone to Pratt, it had been off-limits to the students. One warm Friday in the seventh grade, the girls had a free period and decided to be reckless. They sneaked down the Hill, and planted themselves defiantly on the soft grass at the bottom. Terry, who had decided that she was going to be a palaeontologist some day, was virtuously studying a book on fossils. Julie was beside her, sprawled like a kitten on her side, her hair like a fairy shawl. She was pulling idly at a dandelion, mauve shadows in her eyes.

Terry watched her, with some misgiving. Julie had been looking like that a lot lately, she thought; far away, almost as if she had been spirited into a world that had no room for Terry.

'Really, Julie,' she said firmly. 'Shouldn't you be doing something?'

Julie looked up, languid amusement in her eyes. 'Such as?'

'Preparing for the future,' Terry said stiffly.

Julie laughed. 'I'm not going to go around digging up bones, if that's what you mean.'

'It isn't,' Terry said. 'But honestly, school won't last forever. We're thirteen, and you never seem to think about what's going to come afterwards.'

'Why should I?' Julie asked her.

Terry's face felt hot. Never, never in their eight years of friendship, had Julie brought up the subject of her having money, and Terry's having none.

'You never know,' Terry said stiffly. 'I had a great uncle who was a multimillionaire, and he lost it all in the stock market.'

'All I meant,' Julie added more gently, 'was that there isn't anything I *can* do.'

'That's silly,' Terry told her encouragingly. 'You could be a singer if you worked at it, or a model if you get a little taller, or maybe even a teacher.'

Julie smiled and patted Terry's inky nail-bitten hand. 'Maybe I could,' she said, 'but I don't really want to be any of those things. I guess I don't want to be anything at all.' She rolled dreamily over on to her stomach.

Agitated, Terry tried to return to her tome. A few moments later, the girls heard a rustling in the bushes behind them. They scrambled to their feet and clutched each other. After all, psychopaths had been known to appear in the hills of Los Angeles. But in a moment the rustling ceased, and was replaced by low whispering and grunting. Terry and Julie crept around their tree to look. They saw the head-mistress of the school sprawled out on the rough ground, and on top of her was the new young Puerto Rican janitor. His pulled-down trousers were bunched around his ankles, and when he wriggled his feet to free them, Terry saw the worn soles of his shoes. She and Julie watched in shock for a few moments, then tore away. As Terry ran, she kept hearing the words the headmistress had been saying between gasps, and she felt sick.

Julie was giggling feverishly. 'So *that's* why the Hill is off limits!' she said.

Seeing her pink face and excited eyes, Terry felt even sicker.

Mrs Adams had a house in Palm Springs, and every summer she and Julie spent their weekends there. It was Terry's dream to be asked down also, but it was not until she was fourteen years old that the invitation came. Terry made detailed preparations for the trip. She bought a new bathrobe so that Mrs Adams would think she was chic. Painfully, she pulled out every hair from underneath her arms so that she could go swimming without having to worry. She spent a week's allowance and bought two tiny bottles of 'L'Air du Temps' for her hostesses.

It was fantasy come true, roaring down the freeway towards the adventure, but Terry thought Mrs Adams behaved a little strangely on the ride down. Half the time, she was as excited as a six-year-old child, chattering, pointing out landmarks. But then for long periods she would be silent, resting her head against the limousine window and staring out with expressionless doll eyes. Julie did not act as if anything were amiss and so Terry tried to do the same.

Terry did not have as good a visit as she had expected. Somehow, the strangeness clung. For one thing, the Mohave desert unnerved her – the ominous stretches of sand, always suggestive of travellers lost, dying of thirst, wandering crazed in the moonlight. All the gay shops and restaurants in Palm Springs could not reconcile Terry to those images. And for another thing, the Adams' house made her feel uneasy. It seemed like a ghost house because it was so seldom used. Flash floods had licked away at the foundations, and a graceful lace of sand bordered the floor. There had also been a locust migration several months before, and the edges of the carpet outside Terry and Julie's bedroom was crackly with tiny carcasses. Julie told Terry that this was the house in which her parents had spent their honeymoon; and when Terry found a pair of mildewed men's socks in a drawer, it reinforced her creepy feeling.

Terry tried to be a good guest. She went on the aerial tramway with Julie, shrieked with feigned fear at the swaying, and ate deep dish apple pie in the restaurant at the top. She played tennis at the Racquet Club until her hands were blistered, and went bicycle riding until she fell going down the steep hill on Rose Avenue. She and Julie went in and out

41

of every store on Palm Canyon Drive. They bought romance novels at Bookland, matching sunglasses at Joseph Magnin's, and had three scoops apiece at Baskin & Robbins.

And yet when Sunday night came, the night before they were due to leave, Terry found that she was eager to be getting home again.

They had just come back from Old Las Consuelas, known as the only good Mexican restaurant in town. Terry's stomach was horribly upset, but she was too embarrassed to admit it. She was sitting at the dining-room table, working doggedly on a jigsaw puzzle of Norman Rockwell's 'Harvest Moon'. Julie lay on the floor, her bright hair covering her face, resting. Mrs Adams was smoking a cigarette on the sofa, tense, as if she were waiting for something to happen. She kept going to the bar and nervously jiggling ice cubes as she made herself drinks in heavy Baccarat glasses.

Terry hadn't seen very much of Julie's mother that week. Mrs Adams always seemed to be resting in her room with the door closed. Sometimes, when she and Julie came back from their excursions, Terry would notice that the house looked a little different than it had when they had left, as though people had been there in their absence. It was a little unsettling.

The telephone rang abruptly. Mrs Adams went into her room to answer it. Terry kept up her search for the round-ish puzzle piece with the blue edge. Outside, an eerie hot wind was blowing, as if it were proclaiming revolution in an unknown tongue.

Mrs Adams did not return from her room. Half an hour went by. At last there came a noise, a whimpering cry. 'Julie!'

Julie ran into her mother's bedroom. Terry was left alone with her jigsaw puzzle. After nearly another half-hour, Julie returned. Her eyes were hot and red.

'What is it?' Terry demanded.

'Someone's making Mummy cry.'

Terry took Julie into her arms. Then, in a businesslike way, she went into Mrs Adams' bedroom to see what could be done. Mrs Adams was lying on the bed, swollen-eyed, tousled, hoarse.

'Oh, girls, girls,' she said into the pillow. Her voice was barely intelligible. 'I don't want you ever to grow up. I can't stand for you to be fouled by men.'

The way she said 'men' caused cold goosepimples to run up Terry's arms.

Mrs Adams raised her head from the pillow and looked at the two girls. 'I'm afraid you won't escape it, Terry,' she said mournfully. 'Your little breasts – they've got bigger even since the last time I saw you.'

Horrified, Terry exhaled, trying to shrink her chest.

'Men will be after you soon. But you, my little girl,' Mrs Adams stroked Julie's hair passionately, 'you'll always be safe with Mummy. I'll see to that.'

Julie's lowered eyes told nothing.

Mrs Adams began talking – talking about men. She spoke bitterly about Julie's father. How he had beaten her, how he had humiliated her. She told of the night she had caught him in bed with his manicurist, two weeks after Julie was born. She told of the young Swede with the pale blue eyes who had left her pregnant when she was sixteen. She told of the abortion. She told of movie directors, and the things she had been made to do on lonely locations. She told of women friends betrayed, sucked dry, abandoned, by men. She told and told until four o'clock in the morning.

Julie listened, stoically. Terry listened, sickened. Inside her was an enormous lashing anger. Mrs Adams was right. Men were horrible, men were demons and she would never trust them. But then her thoughts turned to someone with a soft red beard and hands that were never cold. Her Daddy.

'But Mrs Adams,' she said pleadingly, 'surely there are some good men.'

Julie's mother looked at Terry with pity. 'There are no good men,' she said.

Mrs Adams had another drink, then another. To Terry, exhausted as she was, the vodka, the ice cubes, the crystal glass, glittered like daggers. Finally Mrs Adams fell asleep, a shiny line of liquid trailing from her mouth. Terry and Julie pulled the damp satin bedclothes up gingerly around her and went to their own room. They were silent. There was nothing to be said.

Terry washed her face three times that night. She wanted to be pure forever in body and soul. She was filled with a weird euphoria; a sense of purpose. And it was in that moment that she made up her mind. She was never going to be a victim like Mrs Adams. She would never let a man get the better of her, as long as she lived.

'What a mother you have, Julie,' she murmured reverently. 'She'll keep you innocent and safe.'

She did not see the way Julie was looking at her in the mirror. It was the look of a trapped animal.

On a blue September morning, Terry and Julie were in Westwood, getting stationery supplies for their freshman year of high school. Terry was in heaven – she adored all the paraphernalia – crisply blank notebooks, little boxes of lead pencils, slide rules and book covers. It made her feel that school was a great adventure.

A boy was sitting on the steps of the store as they came out. He was Mexican, about fifteen, and very thin. He had dandruff-specked black hair in a ponytail, and a grey T-shirt. Instinctively, Terry started to pull Julie in the other direction.

The boy looked up and saw them. His eyes sparkled when he saw Julie. He gave a low whistle. 'Hey,' he said. 'Foxy little lady. Come to Pepe, pretty lady.'

Julie reared back, clutching against her the shield of notebooks she had just bought. Her face was very pink, and

44

she panted with outrage and excitement. 'You're – disgusting!' she squeaked, and darted around the corner.

Terry spent the night at Julie's house, and all evening long that was all Julie could talk about – the boy and how awful he had been.

At one in the morning, Terry awakened with a jerk. There was a strange shivering in the bed next to her. 'Julie,' she whispered loudly. 'What's wrong? Do you have a chill or something?'

The noise stopped instantly.

They were spending the day at the beach. Julie lay in the sun on a towel that was colour-coordinated to her bikini, and Terry, who burned, did a fair imitation of the Abominable Snowman, covered up with towels, sunscreen and mumu.

'Anyway,' Terry was saying dreamily, 'I figured it all out last night. If you can just pull up that science grade, you'll have a B+ average. If you do well enough in the aptitude tests, you'll have a shot at Stanford. Or USC, at the least. Either's fine with me, really. I'll be a lawyer if I go to Stanford, and an artist if I go to SC. But the important thing is, we'll be together – maybe we can even be room-mates. Wouldn't that be great? Hey, I wonder who we'd talk to about arranging it?'

Julie, behind her dark glasses, had not heard a word. She was gazing out at the sea.

Something was definitely wrong with Julie, Terry thought worriedly as she hung up the 'phone. This was the second Saturday in a row she hadn't wanted to come over. Terry had tried to tempt her with everything she could think of – tree climbing, seeing the Clarks' new litter of kittens, baking muffins – but Julie had said she was sorry but she just didn't feel up to it; that she just wanted to stay at home and be by herself.

'What's the matter with her?' Terry asked her father grumpily.

'Maybe she's growing up.'

'Do you realize,' Terry said dreamily, the morning after Labour Day, 'that tomorrow afternoon we're going to be in high school?'

She and Julie were in Julie's swimming pool. Julie was sitting on the steps in the shallow end, gazing dreamily towards the garden. Terry thought she looked like Hans Anderson's Little Mermaid waiting on her rock in the Copenhagen Harbour. Terry was neck high in the tepid crystal water, vigorously doing the leg lifts that 'Seventeen' magazine had said were guaranteed to remove one inch off her hips.

'High school,' Terry repeated reverently. 'Remember, when we were little we thought the girls in the ninth grade were practically as old as God?'

Julie smiled. 'They used to give us piggy-back rides,' she remembered.

'They used to give *you* piggy-back rides,' Terry corrected. 'They let me walk.' There was a pause as Terry did five more leg lifts, and then she said, 'It'll seem strange, not being children anymore.'

'I don't know about that.' Julie wore a gently mysterious smile. 'I think life is just going to get better and better.'

Terry certainly hoped so. But at the moment it all seemed so uncertain. 'Well, at least we'll always be friends,' she said finally. 'That's one thing for sure.'

She watched Julie sitting with her chin on her hands, dreaming of a future Terry could not see. She looked so beautiful that Terry stared at her in wonder for a long, long time. Finally she whispered something she had never said in all the years they had been friends. 'I love you, Julie.'

Julie said nothing. Terry was not sure she had even heard.

*

Saturday, October third, was Julie's fifteenth birthday and at two o'clock there was going to be a big party at her house.

Terry stood in front of the full-length mirror in her parents' bedroom, whistling, looking with delighted appraisal at her green organza dress. It was the first outfit she had ever made. True, there was something a little erratic about the gathers at the waist, making her look every ounce of her 130 pounds, but the whimsically puffed sleeves pleased her and the bodice was as satisfactorily low-cut as one could wish. If she wasn't going to be the most beautiful guest at today's party, at least she wouldn't disgrace her best friend.

Humming as she dabbed on a bit of Tabu, filched from her mother's dressing table, Terry wondered what Julie would be wearing, what presents she would get, and whether she herself would get on comfortably with the other guests.

Terry sighed. It would have been so much more special if she and Julie could have had a private birthday celebration at Terry's house. But Mrs Adams wouldn't hear of it. Julie had to have the big party, and that was that.

'Terry! For God's sake, hurry up! I've got to get to basketball practice!' bellowed Timmy, who was driving her. But nothing could disturb Terry's mood of serene pleasure. Carefully she gathered together all the birthday presents for Julie that had taken two weeks to select and four weeks' allowance to buy.

'Ready!' she cried happily.

The first indication Terry had that anything was wrong was the painted streamer hanging above Julie's front door, saying 'HAPPY BIRTHDAY'. It was decorated with Raggedy Anne dolls. Puzzled, she rang the bell, and the door was opened immediately by Mrs Adams. She was dressed in a ruffled hostess gown, and looked as flushed and excited and pretty as Terry had ever seen her.

'Come in, dear!' she cried. 'Welcome to my little girl's fifth birthday party!'

Terry walked into the den, in shock. She gasped aloud. A poster of Bozo the Clown was on the wall before her. Paper streamers dangled from the ceiling, and a long table centred in the room had a Peter Rabbit tablecloth on it. There were paper hats, toy horns, and cups of Smarties beside every place. And on the record player, Shirley Temple was demanding animal crackers in her soup.

Terry drew in a shaky breath. Huddled in uneasy little groups were the other guests, saying nothing. Julie was nowhere to be seen. Terry was given a paper cupful of punch by Julie's old nurse. It was so sweet she almost retched.

'Terry, could you come here a moment?' Julie was at the doorway. Her face was white. Terry hurried over and followed her upstairs.

Julie locked them both in her bedroom. She looked at Terry speechlessly. 'I don't know what to do,' she whispered at last. She licked chapped lips. 'I woke up this morning, and there it was. The games. The toys. The decorations. She must have stayed up all night to do it. Oh, God, Terry, could there be something – something wrong with her?'

Julie began to walk crookedly from bed to desk and back to bed again, like a dazed circus animal. 'I told her to take it all down. I tried to explain that I'd rather not have the party at all than to have it like this. But she wouldn't listen.'

The face Julie turned to Terry was terrifying. 'Oh, Terry, what am I going to do?' she begged.

Terry swallowed miserably. She had no answer. Julie fell on to the bed with a bitter sob. There came a knock at the bedroom door, and Mrs Adams' pink, excited voice was calling.

'Girls! Girls! It's time for 'Pin the Tail on the Donkey'!'

*

The next evening, Terry followed her parents into the small Italian restaurant where they loved to go whenever Mr Garvey had had an especially lucrative week at the hardware store. But Terry wished they weren't going tonight, because she couldn't erase from her mind the picture of Julie and her fifteenth birthday party. She followed her parents to their usual corner, feeling as clunky as a scone in her yellow dress. They sat down in the booth and then, cutting through the chatter, was a low snowy voice Terry knew.

A woman was sitting at a table in the back darkness of the restaurant. She was with a blond man. She was very drunk and kept giggling. The sleeves of her dress were pulled down nearly to her elbows, and the pink of her shoulders and breasts shot fiftul gleams into the darkness. She fanned herself with the menu, complaining loudly that the restaurant was too hot. Over and over, she embraced her companion. Her goblet of wine tipped, and she cursed when the red liquid ran sticky, down her chest. The headwaiter came quickly over, his customary aloofness evaporated, as he endeavoured to calm her. She sent him away imperiously. In a few moments she seemed to have forgotten she had ever been angry. She began to kiss her escort with slow, low deep kisses.

Terry and her parents kept talking doggedly about the state of the economy, the state of the front lawn, life at the hardware store, the neighbours' divorce. Not once did they mention Julie Adams' mother making love to the man in the back of the restaurant.

The headmistress climbed heavily on to the auditorium stage. She had become rather stout in the last few years. 'Girls,' she said, 'I have rather a pleasant announcement to make this morning. I have just learned that our Senior Choral Club has been invited to participate in a nationwide competition next month.'

Terry, in the fourth row of the assembly audience, poked

Julie excitedly. Both girls were in the Choral Club.

'Not only that,' the headmistress went on, 'the competition is going to be held in New York City!'

There were cries of delight from the school's musical community, sighs of irritated envy from the others.

'Now, we cannot possibly take everyone in the Chorus, of course, but Miss Finkelstein has asked that the following girls be included . . .' She began to read names from a folded piece of notepaper. Terry found herself growing hot with panicky anticipation, then cold, then hot again. The second to last name on the list was 'Julie Adams', and the last was 'Terry Garvey'.

'I can't believe it!' Terry chattered excitedly to Julie on the telephone that evening. 'My folks are letting me go without a fuss. They're paying for the room at the Plaza and everything! My Dad's getting me a matching suitcase and make-up kit, and Mama's cooking steak tonight to celebrate.' Terry paused delicately. 'How did your mother take the news?'

'She wasn't going to let me go at first,' Julie told her. 'She said New York is too decadent. But she finally gave in. Especially since I explained we'd be sharing a room. She trusts you.'

'Good,' Terry said, relieved. Then she gave a little shriek. 'Can you believe we're actually going to New York? I just can't wait! Boy, have I got plans for us! I got a book out of the library this afternoon, called 'A Thousand and One Things to do in New York City'. We'll be there five days, so I figure if we do only two hundred things a day . . .'

Mrs Adams was there at the airport to say goodbye. 'My little girl will be away from me for the first time in her life,' she said huskily. 'Take good care of her, Terry.'

'I will,' Terry promised staunchly.

Mrs Adams gave Julie a long tender hug. Julie, seeing the

other girls watching, resisted at first, then finally returned the embrace.

The girls giggled.

The Plaza Hotel was wonderful on that October afternoon. Outside, the trees were delicately spare with the touch of autumn. But inside the Palm Court, the tables were jammed and overflowing with guests, flowers, packages. And the messiest table of all was the one at which Terry Garvey and Julie Adams sat.

Terry's mind, stretched taut by all the new experiences of the last three days, was agreeably limp and content now. She leaned back and thought possessively about New York – she was definitely, she decided, a real New Yorker.

Every morning, after choral rehearsal was finished, Terry and Julie were off. The girls were allowed only limited freedom, and were supposed to stay in groups of six, but Terry, the supreme law-abider, lost her head for once, and broke the rules with thoroughness. Eagerly she dragged Julie around to every sight, store and museum that the library book had recommended. Fortunately or unfortunately, Terry had neglected to note that the book had been published five years before, and she found that at least two thirds of the recommended points of interest had gone out of business. But, as Terry kept telling the wan and exhausted Julie, it was all part of the adventure. And even the sights they did see were more than enough. The Metropolitan Museum! Bloomingdale's! The Stage Deli! Terry loved it all.

But perhaps the nicest thing about New York was the Plaza Hotel itself. From the first moment the airport bus had pulled in front, a lump of thrilled delight had come into Terry's throat. The Plaza Hotel had to be the most beautiful building in the world. This belief persisted, even though the heat didn't turn off in her room, the bed was one painful sag, and the bathroom door hung foolishly on its hinges, making it impossible to close.

Julie was less impressed by the hotel, but she loved the

Palm Court. And truly, Terry thought, watching her, Julie did seem to belong in this room – with its air of rosy delicacy and purity.

'I feel we're at Buckingham Palace,' Julie was saying now, smiling.

Terry could not let this inaccuracy pass. 'Oh, no,' she said, her eyes stern behind her spectacles. 'Not Buckingham Palace! Don't you see the curved legs on the chairs? That's French – Louis Fifteenth to be exact – not English.' Terry had now definitely decided she was going to be an interior designer some day.

Julie sighed, dampened. Then suddenly she gasped. 'What time is it? I must call Mummy! I told her I'd call at six. You won't let me forget, will you?'

'Don't worry,' Terry checked her watch. 'It's only 5.30.'

Then the waiter came over, bowed, and insinuated menus into the girls' hands. Julie beamed with bright grey eyes at the myriad delicacies available, then she clutched Terry's arm in a panic. 'Terry! There's a five dollar minimum!'

There was a hurried perusal of handbags to see if they had enough. Julie was the first to find her wallet. She looked inside, and shrieked. 'I've been robbed!'

Every tea-drinker in the Palm Court looked up.

'We've got to go to the police!' Julie panted. 'When could it have happened? In the Park? When that old man bumped us by the bench?'

'What do you mean you've been robbed?' Terry demanded.

Julie's voice was high with despair. 'I mean I had forty dollars this morning, and now I've got three!'

Terry did a few moments' calculation, then she whispered, 'No, you idiot, that's perfectly right. That skirt you bought at Bloomingdale's was seventeen dollars, and entrance to the Frick was two-fifty. Lunch at Zum Zum was three dollars each – '

'And the scarf I bought Mummy was fourteen. Yes, I

guess you're right,' Julie said shamefacedly.

Terry, relieved that the other people had gone back to their pastries, gave Julie a forgiving smile and said that she would pay for them both.

The waiter returned and took their order. Terry gave hers imperiously because she felt awkward. Julie gave hers smiling, then lolled back against the quilted chair with a happy sigh. 'Oh, how I'd love to live in New York some day.'

Terry was terribly taken aback. She did not like to think that Julie was making plans on her own without consulting her. 'You wouldn't last a minute here,' she said firmly. 'You'd get run over by a taxi your first day.'

Julie sighed at the grating tone that had come into Terry's voice. 'I guess you're right,' she said placatingly.

Their eclairs arrived. Terry bit into hers, and declared it was simply the best thing she had ever eaten. Then, almost simultaneously, the trio began to play. And that was the final touch to her contentment. Here she was; free, sophisticated, adventuring – listening to music in the most glamorous room of the most glamorous hotel in the most glamorous city in the world. And sitting next to her was the person she loved most. This was happiness.

Suddenly, Julie's eyes widened, and the colour came up rapidly in her cheeks. 'Terry!' she whispered urgently, 'there are two boys over there behind the plants – and they're *staring* at us!'

Terry's contentment drained away instantly. She gave one startled look, and scowled. The boys were dressed in black leather jackets and jeans, and they were leaning over the railings, peering, grinning through the palms at the diners.

'Just ignore them,' she commanded Julie.

But Julie didn't listen. 'One of them looks so foreign – did you see?' she demanded in a glittering, excited whisper. 'I wonder if he's a Puerto Rican, like in 'West Side Story'.'

'Well, so what if he is?' Terry asked sharply. 'What's it got to do with you?'

'Oh, no!' Julie protested. 'They're coming over here!'

There was an avid rustling behind the two girls now, and suddenly the boys were no longer hidden by the palms. One was sitting by Julie, the other by Terry. The waiter came over quickly to throw them out, but Julie smiled at him with such innocent sweetness that he backed off. Then the girls sat silently, powerlessly, between the boys. It felt a lot different, Terry thought confusedly, to sitting next to her brother. She noticed everything – the blunt over-sized hands, the deep male smell. The tired aroma of the leather jackets and the alarming bulges in their trousers that Julie's mother had warned about.

'What are girls like you doing in a nice place like this?' the dark-skinned boy asked slyly. His voice had a practised sheen to it that Terry found nauseating.

'We're here on business. We're in music,' Julie told him, in a high, breathless sigh.

'Oh, yeah?' The smaller blond boy was interested. 'You girls in a rock group?'

'Yes,' Julie said.

Terry gasped with pained shock. A rock group! Julie caught sight of Terry's expression and looked quickly away. 'And what about you?' she babbled to the boys. 'Do you come here often?'

That was a stupid thing to have said. These greasy gentlemen were far more likely to be regular visitors to a schoolyard basketball court, or the juvenile delinquency court, then the Palm Court.

'I come everywhere, baby,' the dark one said with a smile. 'Listen. Why don't we get out of here? A friend of mine has just opened up a club in the Village. It's terrific. You can do anything you want there.'

Panic began to stir in Terry. She was absolutely unnerved by the way Julie's cheeks had begun to glow at the suggestion. She could not bear it. Something must be done to stop it immediately. Then, as she looked up at the gilded

54

clock in the entrance hall, salvation came.

'It's six o'clock, Julie,' she said in a loud, triumphant voice. 'You have to call your mother.'

'Your *mother*?' the blond boy cackled.

'Why, yes.' Julie told him airily. 'That's what we call the leader of our rock group.'

Terry was so upset by this outrage that she slammed a twenty-dollar bill on the table, instead of a ten, and jumped up from her chair. Julie looked at her, suddenly flustered, and jumped up also. 'I'm sorry – we really do have to go,' she told the boys.

'Hey, are you staying here?' the dark one asked.

Julie paused. 'Yes,' she said finally.

The boy smirked.

'And what names do you go by?'

Terry turned upon Julie the most forbidding scowl she possessed.

'Julie Adams and Terry Garvey,' Julie answered with a glazed smile.

By seven o'clock that evening, the girls were up in their room, in for the night. Three days' worth of clothes were all over the floor, and in a tidy pyramid on the dresser was a wealth of junk food. The television was on, flickering feebly, but neither Julie nor Terry was listening.

Julie was sitting on the vent by the window, the warm air blowing her nightgown in gentle puffs around her. She was smiling dreamily. Terry, hunched miserably in bed, was watching her. She felt so remote from Julie, so sickeningly confused. She wanted to sob and sob.

Julie, as if sensing her feelings, turned around. 'You know what?' she said gently. 'Let's go to Chinatown to-morrow, like you wanted to. Maybe afterwards we can even explore Greenwich Village.'

Relief flowed over Terry's parched nerves at the natural-ness of Julie's tone. No, she thought gratefully, there was no reason to worry. Everything was all right. Everything was normal. What had happened downstairs with those boys – it hadn't been important after all.

'OK,' she said. 'Chinatown and Greenwich Village it is.'

Slowly the two girls smiled at each other. The bad moment was over. And then the theme music of 'I Love Lucy' came on the air.

'Hooray!' Julie shrieked like a five year old, leaping on to the bed with a bounce that made her wild hair soar. And the two girls snuggled under the covers to watch the re-run of their favourite series.

Terry looked over at Julie with her pink Lanz nightgown, her warm freckled skin. This moment, what we have is perfect, she thought passionately. Things must never, never change.

And then the telephone rang.

The two girls looked at each other. The 'phone rang again. Terry looked at it with apprehension. Julie picked it up.

'Hello?'

Even before she looked at her friend's face, Terry knew who was calling.

'Oh, hello,' Julie went on, in that odious breathless voice. 'Really? Up here? Now?'

Terry shot upright from the bed, her fists clenched. 'No,' she commanded. 'Absolutely not.'

On the television, Ricky was telling Lucy that she couldn't come to lunch with him to meet Bill Holden.

'Well . . .' Julie dropped her eyes uncertainly.

'No!' Terry repeated harshly, giving Julie's thin arm a hard shake. 'We're on our honour here – don't you remember? We could be thrown out of Chorus – out of school, even! And do you know what your mother would do if she knew? She'd kill you. And I'll tell her,' she hissed. 'The minute we get home. I swear I will.'

Julie was very frightened now. 'No, don't come up,' she

said hastily, and dropped the telephone receiver so abruptly that it slipped from its cradle and Ma Bell's high, idiotic whine filled the room.

'Did they say they wouldn't come up?' Terry kept badgering her.

'They didn't say anything,' Julie told her stormily.

'But what if they come anyway? We won't let them in, that's all.'

'Of course we won't let them in!' Julie snapped.

But Terry watched her, chilled. For even as Julie spoke, she was walking over to the mirror and starting, slowly and methodically, to brush her hair. Terry willed Julie to stop – but those pale freckled hands continued to pursue their own will, continued to brush, continued to get ready for the arrival of the boys.

Terry felt faint – strengthless. She was being left behind. She was losing Julie. And losing her to boys – horrible, sickening boys. In the mirror behind Julie's reflection, Terry could see her own face. Her own powerless face.

At three-fifteen in the morning, the door opened softly upon the darkened hotel room. Terry, lying sleepless and tense under the covers, opened one tear-sodden eye. She saw Julie bid goodbye to someone in the hallway, then slip inside. In the one moment before the door imprisoned the room in darkness again, Terry caught a glimpse of Julie's face. She almost did not recognize her.

Cautiously, Julie began to feel her way along the wall. Terry watched her with dark-accustomed eyes and feigned the even breaths of a sleeper. Julie reached the bathroom, turned the light on and took off her blouse. Covering the small, firm breasts like scabs, were scores of strawberry marks. Terry stifled a gasp. Julie gave a low half-sigh, half-laugh. Then Terry watched Julie kneel and pull from the bottom of her make-up case a small green and white diary. She began to write.

57

'Julie,' Terry made herself whisper.

The writing stopped.

'Go back to sleep, Terry.'

'What did you do tonight, Julie?'

There was a long pause. Then Julie said evenly, 'Go back to sleep, I said.'

And in that moment, Terry knew she had lost Julie forever.

CHAPTER TWO

Theresa was in her room on the eighteenth floor of the Plaza Hotel, sitting on the chill, anonymous bed. Her head was between her hands, a headache imprisoned there. Behind her closed eyes she could still see the woman with the dandelion hair coming so slowly in the Palm Court.

Theresa sat there, light-headed, exhausted, until the steely autumn sun drained into the river. Finally she made herself look at her watch. It was time to start dressing for the evening's banquet. Resolutely she went into the bathroom and drew a bath. The water began to rush with an obliging thunder into the deep, old-fashioned tub. But it was still not loud enough to drown the knock Theresa knew was coming – the knock which must come.

She straightened up slowly, and shut off the water methodically. The cessation of noise was eerie. She walked to the door and opened it.

'Hello, Terry,' Julie said.

Her voice was still the same. But her face was made up carefully, and no trace of the old freckles was left. On her chin was the small triangular scar she had got falling over a roller skate when she was seven years old.

'Why have you come here?' Theresa whispered.

Julie's head flicked. 'I just thought – so much time had passed.'

Theresa stiffened. As she began to speak, the words jerked from her as though they were being yanked out of her throat by a puppet string. 'Get out,' she said. 'Get out. Get out.'

The marionettes danced over and over again until, her steps harassed and quick, Julie went away.

Theresa waited until Julie had walked back down the hotel corridor and disappeared into the elevator. Then she walked stiffly into her room and meticulously locked the door.

She went into the bathroom. She ran some cold water and began to wash her face furiously. She scrubbed deeper and deeper with the hard cloth. She began to brush her teeth remorselessly until her gums throbbed. She could not calm herself. She was a wind-up toy gone mad. At last she dried her hands and went into the bedroom. She made a 'phone call, cancelling her attendance at the banquet that evening. Again, she blamed it on a headache. She hung up.

This time it was real. It was the worst headache she had ever had. Her temples were two blazing anvils; and over and over a blacksmith was pounding the single word – Julie.

Theresa was too nauseous to take a bath. Her skin seemed to be disintegrating – the nerves exposed. The thought of the hot bathwater touching them was unbearable. She would be burned alive.

Julie. Julie. Keen and sly like a physical blow. Theresa was shivering. She put on her nightgown over her chill body. It was silk Dior, very sheer. Dammit, she thought. Why can't I wear flannel nightgowns like I used to? She lay down on the bed, willing sleep to come quickly. But after only a moment she was in the bathroom, reaching for the bottle of Valium.

Then she got back into bed and pulled the heavy bed-spread, unpleasantly stiff with New York City grime, high around her. Theresa lay tense, waiting for the pounce of sleep.

It was the sun coming, brash and oily, through a chink in the curtains which awakened her. She awoke in panic, her heart racing. She opened her eyes and felt exhausted. Below, she could hear the sounds of taxi drivers, in cheerful Lilliputian warfare beneath her window. The room was hot, and she was still not feeling well. She pulled down the bedspread and felt the perspiration roll down between her breasts.

There had been some dream. *Julie*, she thought. Then she forced her mind away from it.

She sat up carefully and looked at her platinum watch. It was six-thirty. There was work to do. She would concentrate on that. Though not due to attend today's seminar until nine, she would of course be expected to lead the discussion. Theresa looked over at the untouched articles she had meant to get through the evening before. She picked up the first one in the pile.

Julie swam into her mind once again, and once again was drowned.

By eight o'clock, Theresa had finished the articles. She ordered up a pot of coffee from room service, but it was bitter and cold, and she put her cup down after one sip. She felt chilled and emotionless. She moved like a robot.

At eight-thirty, she got dressed. She put on her silk blouse and cream linen suit. Dispassionately she watched the luxurious fabrics slip over the reflection of her taut body in the mirror. How fatiguing the whole process was – selecting clothes, having always to look presentable – and yet, ten years ago, she had been so sure that this would be the ultimate pleasure. Sleek suits, silk blouses – how she had longed to have them. For they, more than anything else, meant Success.

Theresa reached for her make-up, neatly stowed in the Louis Vuitton case. She had bought that case precisely because, fifteen years ago, she had seen a visiting lecturer at Northwestern carrying one just like it. 'I'm going to have one of those, too,' Theresa had vowed. 'One day I'm going to be that successful.' And yesterday morning, when she was checking into the Plaza, she had noticed one of the young receptionists staring at her case in the same way she herself had once stared. For a moment, yesterday morning,

Theresa had wanted to tell that young receptionist – tell her what? she challenged herself. Tell her what, you damned idiot? That it wasn't worth it? Of course it was worth it. Success *was* a good thing. The best. At least it was better than the alternative.

Julie's face seemed to be staring back at Theresa from the mirror.

Theresa found herself rushing with her make-up, rushing to leave the room, rushing to leave behind the thoughts of Julie. She hated her cowardice; but she could not prevent her hands from moving faster and faster, dashing on lipstick, flying with the brush.

At eight forty-five she left the room and hurried down the hall. Her feet felt weak and uncertain beneath her. In the room behind her the 'phone was ringing.

The seminar was over at noon. Weary from too much talking and listening, Theresa left the meeting room and made her way to the revolving door at the front of the hotel. She could make her escape now.

The day had turned out to be very bright. Vendors with vividly painted carts were in the square, selling orange juice, ice cream, shish kebabs, pizza and hamburgers. Shoppers, rested from lunch, hastened with businesslike faces towards the scene of the afternoon's kill. A little boy walked by, hand in hand with his mother, his face aglow with delight as he looked up at her. Seeing him, Theresa smiled involuntarily. Christopher. Christopher used to look at me just like that.

God, I miss him, she thought. If only he were here. Theresa pictured her son's delicate face, his soft blond hair. She could hear his voice, unreliable with hormones, and she ached to be with him. It was too early to call Illinois – he would still be at school. But she would buy him a present, she decided, something ridiculously extravagant. Yes; that's what she would do.

She crossed the frenzied tide of traffic, and walked into F.A.O. Schwartz. She had last gone there with Julie when she was fifteen, and she had remembered it forever afterwards as Paradise. But now, looking around the over-bright and busy store, she saw that the smiling stuffed pandas and giraffes on the shelves were cheap and mass-produced. The Madame Alexander dolls' faces were all the same. And even the Peggy Nisbett figurines, once moulded from porcelain, were now made from plastic. But what did it matter? The children running, frenziedly tugging parents along the length of the store, had no inkling of this drop-off in quality.

There was nothing Theresa cared to buy.

She walked all over the midtown area that afternoon. She found nothing for Christopher. The noise was intense but she did not mind it. Her head was filled with hydraulic drills and honking cabs and her own thoughts no longer seemed to be a part of her. They went as unnoticed as Muzak piped into an elevator, and could no longer hurt her.

For lunch, she stopped at 'Harman's', a luncheonette on 49th Street, and ordered a chicken salad sandwich. It was made with plain chicken and mayonnaise, unadorned by the paprika, grapes, chutney or pineapple favoured by the expensive restaurants she usually frequented. Her mother had made chicken salad sandwiches like these for the family's annual sunset picnic to the beach.

The meal finished, Theresa got up from the booth, leaving a far larger tip than the young waitress was accustomed to getting. Back on the street, as she was putting her Gucci wallet back into her handbag, she found herself roughly bumped.

'I'm so sorry!' A skinny young man in a frayed blazer was peering anxiously at her from behind thick, unstylish glasses. 'Are you all right?'

'Perfectly all right,' Theresa assured him. There was a touchingly wistful quality about the boy – how unexpected to find someone like him on the streets of New York.

He apologized once more, patted Theresa's shoulder as if to comfort it for the ordeal he had put it through, and dashed off again. Theresa looked after him. She guessed he was on his way to a job interview – and she also concluded that he would lose out in favour of some slick, well-dressed over-achiever. That is, unless the personnel director –

'Lady, could you spare some change?'

A bag lady, covered with sores, was holding out a dirty hand. Theresa reached for her wallet. It was gone.

At two o'clock, Theresa was still walking up Madison Avenue. She was numb. She kept telling herself that she was over-reacting – there had only been one hundred dollars in the wallet, after all. The rest of her money and credit cards were safe in the zippered compartment of her handbag. But she felt so violated – and, ridiculously, so disappointed in that young boy.

She reached the Metropolitan Museum of Art, but was suddenly too tired to climb the steps. She just wanted to get back to the hotel.

She tried for a long time to get a taxi, but they sped by without stopping like snide yellow bullets. Theresa began to walk. The afternoon had become overcast, alternately chill and stuffy, and the flashes of sharp, occasional sun made Central Park look gritty and dour. On the benches lining the street was a grim collection. An obese old woman, slumped in a thick black coat, cursed at a pigeon fluttering too near her. A scrawny black man with knotted hair, dressed in nothing but red satin boxing shorts, laughed and chatted affectionately to himself. A young boy whose face showed pain even as he slept, clutched at the bars of his bench as if it were a prison window.

Theresa walked by them all. She felt nothing. The only pain she felt was the blister rising up inexorably on her heel. The poverty, the insanity, the misery of these other people –

what were they to her? And that she could feel this way made her afraid.

On the next bench was a ragged, empty-faced woman with a child butting miserably against her legs. Theresa stopped. She opened her change purse and gave the woman its contents. The mother thanked her, babbling with gratitude, but even that basic act of giving and receiving did not cause any warmth of feeling to flow into Theresa. She felt like an astronaut out in space, at the end of a tether. I am completely alone, she thought as she walked back to the hotel. Completely alone.

By the time Theresa at last reached the Plaza, an uneasy drizzle had begun to fall. As she came through the lobby, she could hear the strains of the trio in the Palm Court, and she hurried away from it. She took the brass elevator up to the eighteenth floor and went down the hall to her room.

She stared around, disoriented. Nothing looked familiar. Not the suits she could see reflected in the mirror of the open wardrobe, not her Louis Vuitton make-up case. Theresa had the odd fancy that they were all items belonging to a stranger – a stranger who was going to put her key in the lock in a moment, open the door, and scream at Theresa for being a trespasser.

Christopher, she thought suddenly; and a sense of belonging returned. I'll call Christopher. It's late enough now – he'll be home from school.

She dialled the number eagerly. Christopher answered on the fifth ring. 'Hi, my pumpkin,' she said. She hadn't used that nickname in years.

There was a pause. 'Hi, my pumpkin?' Christopher asked. 'Who's calling – Cinderella?' Behind him Theresa could hear the rough laughter of other boys.

'Who's there?' she asked, stung by the way she had spoken.

'Just some of the guys,' he said sullenly.

She stiffened. 'I thought I had made that clear – no friends after school until those history grades pick up.'

'Well, I forgot,' he said. 'I guess I don't have a stellar brain like you, Mom.'

'Don't be so flip, Christopher,' she burst out. 'This is serious. We made a bargain, and I expected you to keep it.' She paused. This was not the way she wanted to speak to him. This was not why she had called. 'How's everything going?' she tried again.

'Okay.'

'How did the French test go? Did you tell the gym teacher about that knee?'

'No.' he said. 'I guess I forgot that, too.'

She let it pass. 'Is Mrs Phillips feeding you real food, or are you getting high on hamburgers?'

He did not answer.

'Come on, Chris!' Theresa could hear the boys in the background. 'Look, Mom,' Christopher said. 'I've got to go.'

'In one minute,' she said. 'I wanted to tell you about my trip. There was this one woman in this morning's seminar, and you'll never guess what she asked me.'

'Mom,' he said, 'the guys are dragging me out.'

Theresa closed her eyes. Damn the guys, she thought. Damn the guys for dragging my son away from me. 'Christopher,' she said sharply. 'I miss you a lot.'

He was silent. She couldn't help herself. 'Do you miss me?' she pursued.

And then she heard a girl's silly laugh on the other end. 'Christopher,' she demanded, 'is there a girl over there?'

'Oh, Mom,' he said angrily. 'You always get things wrong.'

'I just want to know what you're doing,' she said hotly.

'Having an orgy, Mom – what else?'

Theresa could hear the room explode with laughter. She felt herself flushing. 'That's enough, Christopher,' she said.

'I will not have you talk to me like this.'

'Mom,' he said, 'You were the one who wanted to talk in the first place – not me.' And he hung up.

Theresa sat on the bed, looking stupidly at the dead 'phone. Oh, God, she thought. Who do I think I am, telling mothers how to raise their children? When all the time my own son hates me.

Don't be a fool, she told herself sharply. He doesn't hate me. He's just growing up. '*Julie's just growing up,*' came her father's voice from the long past. Julie! Julie!

So it seemed they all grew up and left her.

Oh, Christopher; oh, my darling, Theresa thought, picturing the soft feathers of hair at the base of his head. I love you so much, and you're all I have.

She covered her face with her hands. They felt like the uncaring hands of a stranger.

CHAPTER THREE

The rumours about Julie began to circulate soon after the Choral Club's return from New York. The general verdict was that she had completely changed – some girls thought for the better, some for the worse. But she was no longer under the thumb of Terry Garvey, that was for certain.

When Julie was publicly chastised by the headmistress for wearing skirts three inches shorter than the school uniform code allowed, the rumours snowballed. One girl claimed to have seen Julie smoking pot in the bathroom. Another said her sister had seen Julie at Alice's Restaurant when she was supposed to be in Study Hall. Another said she was sure she was dying her hair. Sweet, innocent little Julie!

The girls did not share with Terry any of the gossip, sensing that she would not be pleased to hear it. But instinctively, Terry managed to find it all out. She did not know how she felt about what was going on with Julie. Sad, mainly. Very, very sad.

One afternoon, Terry took the short cut across the gym field on her way to her eighth period biology class. As she passed the gateposts at the entrance to the school, she caught sight of Julie, and stopped. Julie was sitting on the low concrete post, facing the street. Her kneesocks and shoes were in her hand. She looked like a little child – and also like a woman. Her long hair was freed of its barrette and poured down her back, and she sat at her ease, smiling, stretching like a cat in the sun. Terry hid in the shadow of the bleachers and watched.

There was a noise from the street. A red Volkswagen

pulled up to the kerb in front of the school. Terry could dimly make out a blond boy at the wheel. Julie came down languorously from her concrete pedestal and got inside. The car drove away. Soon everything was silent again. Terry paused for a moment, and then ran to her biology class.

The boy in the Volkswagen pulled Julie to him and kissed her. 'I've missed you,' he said.

She smiled but did not answer.

Terry was very lonely the fall of her senior year. Because she had always had Julie, she had never really bothered making other friends – and now that Julie was out of her life, it seemed hypocritical to try and start getting close to the other girls. And as far as boys were concerned, Terry had not budged from that long-ago decision in Palm Springs that men brought you nothing but betrayal and disillusion, and that she would never allow one in her life.

So she concentrated on her schoolwork.

One hot October afternoon, Terry was at the Brentwood library, looking through the list of books she would need for her term paper on the Hundred Years' War. She walked over to the appropriate stacks and touched each volume lingeringly before pulling it out.

Terry loved libraries. She found such peace there, in the busy quiet flow of concentration.

When the nine huge books had been collected, Terry hoisted them into a graduated pile, and began to stagger forward to the check-out counter. But halfway across the room, the pyramid began to collapse. Terry gasped. The books started swaying feverishly in her arms. She clutched. She squatted. The volumes veered to the left, then the right.

Terry was choked with humiliation. She dug in with her elbows, her knees, her chin; anything to keep the fifty pounds of books from collapsing with a gigantic boom on to the library floor. For nearly a minute, she stood clenched in hunchbacked agony, while all around her people put down their work and watched with amusement.

Then suddenly, someone was taking the books gently away.

It was a boy. He had dark blond hair and tanned skin that looked warm to the touch. He wore a plaid shirt that had faded to nursery colours, and his eyes were olive-green. He smiled at Terry. He was undeniably a very beautiful boy. All nine books were in his arms now – and he was carrying them effortlessly to the check-out counter.

'Honestly, you don't have to do that – I could have managed,' Terry whispered. But the boy only shook his head, smiling. Soon the books were checked out, and the encounter was over. And Terry found, to her great surprise, that she wished it could be prolonged.

To her delight, it happened.

'Is someone giving you a lift home with these, Miss Theresa R. Garvey?'

Terry blushed to think that he had taken the trouble to notice her name on the library card.

'No, but it's really all right,' she fussed self-consciously. 'I live only a few blocks from here.'

The boy laughed. 'You'll never even make it down the steps. Why don't you let me help?'

Those green eyes looked so comforting and kind. Terry couldn't believe the feelings that were creeping through her. 'Well, all right,' she mumbled.

She was Scarlett O'Garvey.

The two of them walked half a block in silence on the dusty, heat-teased sidewalk.

'I'm Michael Spenser, by the way,' the boy said at last.

She only nodded shyly. Michael was her favourite name, but she didn't tell him so.

'Are you studying for an exam?' he tried again, nodding at the books.

70

'No.' Terry and witty repartee seemed hopelessly estranged that afternooon. 'These are for a thesis. One hundred books on the One Hundred Years' War.'

'What school do you go to?'

'Pratt.'

He was silent a long time. Terry wondered anxiously if she had said anything wrong. 'I know – I knew a girl at Pratt,' he said at last, almost unwillingly. He did not offer the girl's name, and Terry, alerted by something in his voice, did not ask. Instead, as they walked the rest of the way to her house, she made an extensive mental review of all those 'Cosmopolitan' and 'Sixteen' magazine articles she had jeered at as late as the week before – articles on How to Talk to Men. Fervently, she asked Michael about his school, his interests, his plans. She was glad to hear that he wanted to be a research doctor and that he was interested in fighting diseases, not making money. But she was less pleased to hear that he had applied, early admission, to Northwestern University. Chicago was two thousand miles away.

Her questions continued. Terry learned that Michael's father was a salesman and his mother a housewife. There were three younger sisters. One of them was going to be a nun. The whole family went camping every June, and right now they were building a catamaran in the backyard.

'And what else do you do for fun?' Terry asked.

'Oh, the usual things. I go to movies a lot.'

'So do I.' Terry smiled at the coincidence. 'Who's your favourite actor?'

'Richard Burton, I guess.'

She was stunned. 'Mine, too!' Terry let this extraordinary similarity of tastes sink in a moment, then she added eagerly, 'You know, they're showing 'Cleopatra', down in Santa Monica next week.'

The moment she said it, she knew what a terrible mistake it had been.

'Look, Terry,' Michael said awkwardly, after a long

silence. 'I just got over what I thought was a serious relationship, see, and – no offence meant – but I don't really think I'm up to dating anyone else right now.'

Terry went limp with humiliation. To think she had been soliciting a *date*! She continued to chatter madly, no longer along the lines advised by 'Cosmopolitan', but about anything – anything that would take even a few seconds off the now-endless walk home. She told Michael about her school, her parents, summer camp, even about sightseeing in New York with Julie.

'Julie?' Michael asked.

'A girl called Julie Adams. She used to be my best friend.'

They had reached Terry's block now, and in silence they approached her house. Terry held out her arms for the books, a huge miserable smile on her face. 'Well – thank you again,' she said.

They looked at each other a moment.

'Listen, Terry,' Michael said suddenly. There was an odd glimmer in his look. 'If your Hundred Years' War cools off a little, maybe we could see 'Cleopatra' next week after all. What's your number? I'll give you a call.'

Terry waited until he had turned the corner before throwing all nine books on the ground and screaming with ecstasy.

From time to time that fall, Terry thought of Mrs Adams and her theories about men. Thought of them with such kind pity.

On a misty November afternoon, Terry parked her mother's green station wagon in an alley behind Michael's street and crept to the spot by his driveway where the bushes were thickest. It was a good hiding place. She could see the house clearly, but couldn't be seen herself. Her heart skipped like an excited child playing a spy game. It thrilled her to be so close to Michael, without his knowing she was there.

The whole family was in the backyard. Terry studied them so eagerly her eyes smarted behind her contact lenses. There was Michael's father, making compost. He looked rather grim – almost too unfriendly to be a salesman. And Michael's mother – how tiny she was. Terry noticed that one foot trailed behind the other as she gathered together bags of leaves. Michael hadn't told her that his mother was lame. That touched Terry very much.

And there was Michael. He was wearing the plaid shirt she loved. How strong and spare he looked raking over flowerbeds on this ragged November day. Like a woodcut of a farmer – no, Thoreau – working the land. Terry's heart beat tears into her eyes.

Time passed. It was getting cold inside her bush. She couldn't stay there indefinitely. Terry wondered if she had the nerve just to go up to the house casually, say she was passing by, and invite herself in. But she knew she didn't. Soon the garden work was finished, and the family went back inside the house.

Terry sneaked away and drove home, exhilarated.

Being in love was not at all what Terry had imagined. Rather than being ennobling and dramatic, it was made up of an all-encompassing tenderness and aching poignancy. She was willing to do anything for Michael, anything that would bring softness and pleasure to his life. She wanted to absorb him, be absorbed by him. Sometimes, after a date, she would lie in bed and try to link her thoughts with Michael's, the way the lovers did in 'Peter Ibbetson', but it never worked.

That worried her a little. And it also worried her that sometimes, on a date, after she and Michael had discussed the movie they had seen, and what had happened in school that day, conversation ran out. Michael would just sit there, and make no effort to talk.

Give him time, she would tell herself. Michael was just a

very quiet, shy boy. He had had a cold childhood. No one had ever cared the way she cared. He just wasn't used to being loved. But one day, one day he would reveal everything to her. All of himself. And in the meantime, what did it matter? She knew she loved him, and that was enough.

It was night. Terry and Michael were taking a walk through the shadowy streets of Van Nuys. It was late November, and a mournful stillness kept watch on the suburban streets.

Terry and Michael passed under a streetlamp and their two shadows, his shadow's arm around her shadow's shoulder, filled her with a great glorious sense of fate revealing itself.

'Do you tell your friends about the two of us?' Michael asked suddenly. 'I mean about how happy we are?'

'No,' Terry said. 'What about you?'

'I don't have a lot of friends to tell,' Michael shrugged.

'Me, neither,' Terry told him. 'You're my only friend.'

'But didn't you used to have a best friend?' he asked after a pause. 'Some girl you told me about the first time we met?'

'Oh. Julie. No, I don't see much of her these days.'

They walked along in silence for a while, and then Terry stopped. 'But we are happy,' she said. It was almost a question.

'Of course we are. Why? What's the matter?'

Terry felt horribly uncomfortable. She had never voiced this worry before, not even to herself. 'Well, it's just that . . . You've never once tried to . . . I mean, you do find me attractive, don't you?'

'Oh, sure, Terry,' Michael said quickly. 'I just have a lot of respect for you, that's all.'

'Oh.'

They resumed walking and then Terry stopped again. 'I've made you forget all about that other girl, haven't I? The one you broke up with before you met me?' Under the streetlamp, her face was wistful.

'Of course you have, Terry.' Michael leaned down and gave her a gentle kiss. 'Of course you have.'

One Saturday Terry walked into Bullocks Westwood, and there was Julie at the perfume counter. The girls saw each other at the same moment, so there was no avoiding the greeting.

'Hello, Julie.' Terry walked over with an awkward smile.

'Hello,' Julie said.

'Buying some perfume, I see,' Terry commented. 'Paco Rabanne. Isn't that for a man?'

'Yes,' Julie said with a strange little smile, then added, 'I hear you got an A in that last calculus test. Boy, that's some achievement. It was a killer.'

'Well, you know me,' Terry said. 'I always did over-study.' She fished about furiously for something to say next, something to take the awkwardness away. For a second, she even thought of telling Julie about Michael – maybe that would make Julie feel more at ease with her, knowing that Terry, too, had someone to buy Paco Rabanne for, if she wished. But she didn't. Michael was too precious to be used as small talk.

'How's your mother?' she asked finally.

'Just fine. And your family?'

'Just great. Timmy met a girl at SC and may be getting married!'

'Unbelievable.'

The saleslady came back with the wrapped perfume and handed it to Julie.

Terry waited until Julie had signed the charge card. 'We really must get together sometime,' she said.

'Oh, absolutely,' Julie agreed, without looking at her. 'Give me a call some day when you're free.'

'I sure will,' Terry said. 'Well, I'd better be going now. I'm trying to find a halfway decent handbag.'

'Good luck,' Julie said. 'Goodbye.'

As Terry walked away, she felt such a dragging sense of loss. She tried to cheer herself up by thinking of Michael, and by remembering that she didn't need Julie anymore, but the terrible depression stayed with her. She left Bullocks without looking for the new handbag after all.

After her visit to the Spensers via the front bushes, Terry asked Michael every time they went out when she was going to meet his parents. She felt somehow that once she met them, she and Michael would be established as a team for good. Then a week before Christmas, the invitation finally came.

Panicked by the thought of arriving late, Terry had left home forty-five minutes early, and was now circling Michael's block for the thirty-seventh time. Every few minutes she would pull over to the side of the road, tilt down the mirror and look at herself in despair. Two pimples and badly-trimmed bangs. That was all she could see. That would be all Michael's parents would see, too. Dear God!

Exactly at seven o'clock, the car radio began to play 'Silhouettes on the Shade', her favourite song. It was a good omen – the best possible! It gave Terry the courage to pull up firmly in Michael's driveway and open the car door. This was as far as she got for some minutes, for she discovered that during her innumerable turns around the block, the Christmas presents she had bought for his family had spilled over the back seat. As gracefully as she could, Terry crawled all over the floor to gather them up, hoping that no one was watching from the house.

At last she staggered to the front door, and there was Michael. He took the presents gently from her arms, much as he had relieved her of the nine books at the library.

But that was to be the last pleasant moment in the evening.

'Terry?' Michael's mother came to the door. She was

76

wearing jeans and an embroidered Mexican shirt, and she smiled curiously at the green velvet skirt and pink blouse that Terry, wanting to be festive, had worn.

She looked at the pile of the gifts. 'You shouldn't have done that,' she said. People were always saying that – but Terry realized with a chill that this woman meant it.

The house was ghastly, decorated with muddy colours and sad with neglect. The only thing that shone gaily was the enormous colour television set in the living room. Terry struggled wildly to find compliments – she praised an embroidered pillow, demanded to know where a certain firescreen had been found, and asked for a tour of the rest of the house. Mrs Spenser said matter-of-factly that everything had been bought at the May Company, on sale, and that a tour was pointless, because all the rooms looked about the same.

The rest of the family came downstairs. On the drive over, Terry had rehearsed again and again her opening lines to each. To Mr Spenser the boat-lover, she was going to mention an article she had read in the *L.A. Times* Leisure Section about catamarans. Dena she was going to ask when she had first felt the religious call. To Karen, the sister Michael had dubbed materialistic, she was going to say, 'I love the shoes (dress, trousersuit) you're wearing.' And to little Jamie who, from all that Michael had told her, was Terry's favourite, she was simply going to say, 'I've been wanting to meet you so much.'

But when Terry shook Mr Spenser's hand, she was so alarmed by his sour face that she forgot her catamaran line – and the sisters, including Jamie, looked at her with such a mixture of amusement and malice that Terry could only mumble hello.

'Would you like a drink before dinner?'

Terry decided it would be wise not to ask for anything alcoholic. 'I'd like some club soda, if you have it,' she said.

She was told they didn't.

'Then any kind of diet soft drink.'

'We only have Coke,' Mrs Spenser said. 'None of us is on a diet.'

The family grouped itself on the shabby brown and gold plaid upholstered furniture and looked at Terry.

'I understand you want to be an architect,' Mr Spenser said.

'That's right,' Terry told him eagerly, glad of the chance to appear in a flattering light.

No one said anything.

'Terry's going to be a great architect,' Michael rushed in. 'She's the most ambitious girl I've ever met.'

Mrs Spenser raised her eyebrows so pointedly at this that, even as her heart took a suicidal dive, Terry couldn't help asking, 'Is anything wrong, Mrs Spenser?'

'Oh, no,' the woman said in a faraway voice. 'Though I must admit I've never seen the point of women working outside the home. To me, running a house has always been perfectly fulfilling. But I'm probably just old-fashioned.'

Terry was aghast. 'Oh, my goodness no! There's nothing wrong in being a housewife!' she said quickly.

There was an expressive pause.

'Why, thank you,' Mrs Spenser said drily.

Dinner was a disaster. The main course was broiled fillet of sole and Terry hated fish. So with the cleverness of desperation, she cut the sole into tiny bites which she camouflaged under her string beans.

'This fish is so delicious,' she told Michael's mother brightly. 'You must give me the recipe.'

'You haven't eaten a bite,' Mrs Spenser said, and, lifting up the string beans, disclosed the entire cache of uneaten fish.

Terry cringed. 'I guess I'm just a little too nervous to eat,' she faltered.

She did not like the triumph in Mrs Spenser's eyes.

Terry did not say a word through the rest of the meal. She

listened to the others talk and laugh. Their conversation was enviably cross-hatched with secret jokes and private histories, and not for an instant was she allowed in. Michael, dear Michael, tried hard to include her. He told everyone about her straight A average, about her terrific singing voice and her really great brownies. But Terry felt the sick doom.

When the meal was over, Terry leaped to her feet like a homemaker born and bred and begged to be allowed to clear the table. She was granted permission, and broke the salad bowl. And when she came out of the kitchen, drying reddened hands, the Spensers' golden retriever leaped up and left two muddy paw prints on a most personal part of Terry's anatomy.

At last it was time to go home. Michael walked Terry to her car at the end of the evening. Neither of them said anything.

In January, Terry's first semester report card arrived, and Mr and Mrs Garvey were dismayed by their daughter's badly-fallen grades. They asked her repeatedly if something was wrong. Terry honestly replied that nothing was. Nevertheless, Terry's parents announced a new rule – that until her grades improved, Terry could leave the house at night only on weekends.

One Wednesday evening she was caught by her mother, sneaking out of the kitchen door.

'This can't go on,' Mrs Garvey said.

Terry had never been close to her mother in her life, and she looked on her interference now with writhing anger. 'Yes, it can,' she said evenly.

Terry thought she was going to be slapped, but Mrs Garvey only sat down at the kitchen table. Terry was surprised to see how heavily her mother slumped into the chair – as if she had been made strengthless.

'Terry, do you know what this could mean if it keeps on?'

she asked in a low voice. 'All your plans – going to Stanford, being an architect – they're all in danger because of this boy.'

Terry had had no idea her mother had even known about Michael. Mrs Garvey looked so bewildered, younger than her daughter had ever seen her look in her life.

'Don't worry, Little Mother,' she said, using a name lost since childhood. 'Don't worry. I'm still going to college, and I'm still going to make the family fortune. You know I'd never let you or Daddy down.'

And she went out to meet Michael.

It was a coldblooded Saturday in late January. Terry drove over to Michael's house. When she pulled into the cracked asphalt driveway, the front door of the ranch house was yanked open and Michael came outside, hopping with cold in his thin sweater. He was flapping a letter.

'Northwestern!' he hollered. She could hear him even through the closed car window. 'I'm in!'

Terry continued to park the car, mechanically and methodically. Then slowly she got out. Michael dashed over and gave her a tremendous, child-like hug. He was more excited than she had ever imagined he could be. She began feeling a succession of cold blows in her stomach.

He drew her inside the house and showed her, over and over, the letter of acceptance, the admission form, the enclosed brochure about dormitories for freshmen.

'Wait till you see the stadium! It's one of the largest in the country,' he told her, his green eyes blissful. 'And if I do OK as a pre-med, I've got a good chance for the Med. School!'

'How could you not do well?' Terry asked politely, in a stiff, dry voice. The blows in her stomach threatened to kill her.

She went over to a cracked leather chair whose stuffing was held back by masking tape, and sat down. Michael noticed her quietness. He tried to talk about other things, but in the end he was always led back to Northwestern.

'We really ought to celebrate,' he said. 'My parents are out – there's some wine in the cabinet.' He got the wine and poured it, and they drank. He toasted Northwestern, the greatest college in America, and they drank again.

Terry stared at Michael's rough gold hair, the tanned broad hands. He was so blindingly precious to her. And he had no idea how his victorious little boy smile and eager talk of college were ripping away at her heart. He was leaving her. That was all there was room for in Terry's brain. Separated – they would be separated.

She couldn't bear it. A buzzing began in her head. Ugly hot tears splashed down her face.

'Hey – what's the matter?'

'Please,' she whispered. 'Would you hold me?'

Obligingly Michael held her on the cracked leather chair. 'What's wrong?' he asked, concerned. 'Are you sure you're OK?'

The puzzlement in Michael's voice was unbearable to Terry. Didn't he realize at all what his going to college meant? Hadn't he given any thought to her at all? She thought of empty years – forever without him. They crashed in an unmuffled drumbeat against her.

'Please. Please! Just keep holding me!'

His arms tightened, and then Terry could not believe what she was doing. She was grabbing Michael, kissing him fiercely, wildly, the way she had never kissed him before, the way she had always dreamed of kissing him. She was sobbing, caressing him, crying out wild things – things she never imagined she could say. And Michael started to respond.

When the point came where Terry could no longer stop it, she was glad. She welcomed it, fiercely. And she welcomed the pain. It proved she was real – real and not an insubstantial shadow. She had found the way to beat Northwestern. She had found the way to make Michael close to her.

For a few moments at least, he belonged to her completely.

Michael seemed to know what Terry was going to tell him before she was halfway through the door.

'No,' he said. 'Oh, Terry, no.' He turned from her, sat down on the chair secured with masking tape, and put his head between his broad hands.

She went to him. 'It's all right,' she whispered. 'I mean, we love each other. We love each other so much. And we would have got married eventually, wouldn't we?'

He lifted his face. His eyes were blank. 'You want to get married?' he asked dully.

The colour in Terry's face rose and fell like an elevator gone mad. 'Why, of – of course,' she whispered.

He stood up and began to walk distractedly around the room. 'You don't know what this means,' he said bitterly. 'This changes all my plans.'

Terry straightened up, and a look came over her face that was unlike any she had ever given Michael before. 'And what about *my* plans?' she asked in a low voice. 'What does all this mean for me?' Then the tension trembled out of her voice, and she went to him, clung to him. 'Oh, Michael, everything's going to be all right,' she told him unsteadily, 'Nothing has really changed. You'll still be a doctor, you'll still go to Northwestern – only now I'll be there with you, that's all.' She laughed nervously. 'Me and the baby, I guess I should say.'

He didn't speak at all. She touched his hair. 'I so want it to be a boy,' she whispered. 'A boy who looks just like you. Can't you just picture him with his – '

Michael stiffened and slid from her embrace. 'My God!' he cried. 'Stop it, Terry.'

She crumpled on the sofa and began to sob. 'Say it's going to be all right, Michael,' she kept pleading. 'Say it's going to be all right. Say it. Say it.'

He sat back down on the chair and put his hands over his

face again. But through his open fingers he could still see her lying there.

Terry's parents were in the den watching 'The Patty Duke Show' when she came through the door. The volume was on very high because Terry's father was going a little deaf. Terry's heart caught. Her parents seemed so very vulnerable sitting there on the worn sofa. Her mother looked so tired, her father so thin. Terry wondered how long it had been since she had really looked at them. She wondered how long it had been since she had really looked at anyone except Michael.

'Come and sit down,' Mr Garvey smiled at her. 'Patty's really got herself into a fix this time.'

Terry watched the screen, unseeing, wishing that the life on the television were the real one, and her own the made-up story. She waited until the commercial.

'There's something I want to tell you,' she said. At her tone, her mother dropped her sewing. Her father slowly looked away from the set. 'I'm going to have a baby,' Terry said. 'And Michael and I are going to get married.'

For a long time there was such frozen stillness that Terry thought her parents hadn't heard. Then she realized that her mother's hands were inching up and sawing stiffly at her throat. 'Oh, God, no.' So soft it was like a sigh from the curtains. 'Oh, God, no.' Louder, final, like the window breaking in a storm.

'It's all right,' Terry said sharply. 'We love each other.' And that made everything all right.

She swallowed. Behind her, on the television, Mrs Olsen comforted a heartbroken young wife who could not seem to make a good cup of coffee. 'Listen,' Terry said loudly. 'You think I won't go on to college now, or have a career. Well, that's just nonsense. Of course I will. Nothing's changed. I'm still going to make the family fortune, and don't you forget it.' She forced a laugh. 'It'll just have to be put off a little, that's all.'

Mrs Garvey closed her blue-veined eyelids and smiled. It was the most horrible smile Terry had ever seen. It made her want to scream and scream and run to her parents like a child crying to be delivered from a nightmare. But her feet didn't move. That smile must go on, and her own cheery, desperate voice. Must go on forever.

'Go on now, finish watching the show,' she said. 'I think there's hope for Patty after all. Don't you?'

Julie stood in her chemise, getting ready for Terry's wedding. Her face was very still. She began applying make-up to her cheeks. Her face pinkened, softened, under each stroke. She put on eye shadow. The eyes took on life.

Julie put the make-up down, and went over to her bed. On it was large blue box from Tiffany. She untied the white ribbon and drew out the crystal vase that was her wedding present to Terry and to Michael.

She lifted it up and smashed it as hard as she could against the wall.

Theresa Rose Garvey and Michael Elliot Spenser were married on July the twentieth at the Episcopal Church in Beverly Hills. It was a small affair, as many of the people invited were away on summer vacation.

Terry had asked Michael if they could write their own service, but he said he was not up to it.

Terry's gown was from Saks. It was loosely cut in the waist.

The reception was held in the Escoffier Room at the Beverly Hilton. Terry's uncle was the assistant manager and he got the Garveys a good price. There was a buffet table and a band and flowers and dancing. Terry asked Michael to dance with her eighty-three-year-old grandmother, but again, he said he just didn't feel up to it.

Michael's family did not come to the wedding. Terry

explained to everyone that they lived out-of-state and couldn't afford to come.

At six o'clock, Terry and Michael left for Tijuana in Michael's Volkswagen beetle that his parents had agreed to sell to him. Terry's brother Timmy tied old tin cans to the bumper.

As they drove away, Terry turned to Michael. Her mascara was edging her cheeks with thick black bars. 'I'm going to make you very happy,' she said.

After the honeymoon, on the first day of her real married life, Terry woke up at six-forty-five in the morning, chilly and scared. It was hard to believe that when she opened her eyes she wouldn't be seeing the little motel room in Tijuana and the sweet, childish sunlight coming in through the slatted blinds. Today wouldn't be yet another carefree day of swimming and shopping and having fun little adventures. Those days were over.

Terry finally got up the courage to open her eyes. What she saw was a small, white bare room, leading to another small, bare white room. There was no heat in the new apartment yet, so it was damp and cold. By the bed, still unpacked, were the two suitcases they had taken on the honeymoon. Terry and Michael had got in very late the night before and had been too tired to do the job then. Seeing the valises now, Terry stifled a panicky sob.

'Michael!' She shook his warm naked shoulder gently, and then more firmly.

'What is it?' He shot up to a sitting position, rubbing his eyes like a perplexed little boy. 'The alarm hasn't gone off. What are you waking me for?'

He lay back down again. Terry pressed her cold front to his warm back, trying to fit herself into all his curves. 'I'm scared,' she whispered. 'I want to be still on the honeymoon.'

Michael was annoyed. 'You woke me up to tell me that?'

he asked incredulously, and went back to sleep.

Coffee, Terry told herself firmly. I'll feel better when I've had some coffee. She got out of bed, and took out her new pink robe from the smaller suitcase. The smell of coconut tanning oil still on it made her sigh. Then she went resolutely to the kitchenette. There was no coffee. There was no pot. There were no mugs. Of course not. The boxes of supplies hadn't arrived from Los Angeles yet. All there was in the kitchen were the glaringly white appliances and some awful curtains with tomatoes on them. Terry's gaze became fixed to these until she couldn't get free. She knew that, from this moment on, she was going to hate tomatoes all her life.

The panicky feeling began to come again. It felt like the first day at summer camp, the first night she had ever spent away from home. But that was ridiculous. It wasn't really like that at all. She was a woman now, married to a man she adored, expecting a baby, and setting up house in her own apartment in an exciting new town. She was incredibly lucky.

She hadn't been able to see much of Evanston on the drive last night, but she remembered the way Michael had raved about it, the day he had been accepted at Northwestern. How bright and free from dust all the trees were, compared with Los Angeles. How homey and pleasant all the people seemed – even the policemen were friendly.

Feeling a little more courageous, Terry drew the tomato-decked curtain aside and looked out hopefully. She saw a lot of small, grubby apartment buildings, each painted in a different dingy pastel. The whole block looked like a line of badly washed coloured sheets hung out to dry. She also saw dustbins, the same as back in California, a dispirited little park, and a few people, mainly older men, who looked about as glum as the old men back home. Terry let the curtain drop.

From behind her came a creaking and a stirring in the

bedroom. Michael was awake. He came out looking tired and peevish, and not at all the way he had looked in Mexico.

Terry flew to him. 'Good morning, my darling!' she cried, but he did not respond.

'I couldn't get back to sleep after you woke me up,' he complained. She felt stricken. Oh, no; he was in a bad mood. Please, she begged God, don't let this happen. Not on the first day of our real married life.

She did not answer him, just changed the subject. 'I was wondering what to give you for breakfast,' she said hastily. 'We don't seem to have anything.'

'Oh, don't worry about that,' Michael told her. 'I'll skip breakfast today. I want to get to school early to register, anyway.'

'Oh,' Terry said.

She sat by the tomato window while Michael dressed in the bedroom. She thought every noise he made sounded eager, as if he couldn't wait to leave her. She told herself not to be so silly. He came out finally, looking boyish and soft from shaving.

'Well? How do I look?'

Her heart trembled like jelly with love for him. 'You look beautiful,' she said so fervently that her teeth almost chattered. 'Just so beautiful.' And she went to him for a kiss. He kissed her, but a bit more quickly than she would have liked.

He gathered together paper, folders. His face was remote, his mind was already on the day ahead. As he was getting ready to leave, he asked politely, 'And what are your plans for today?'

Pride made Terry conceal the truth – that she would spend the day waiting for his return. 'Oh, I'll get to know the neighbourhood,' she said airily. 'Maybe even knock on a few doors and meet some of the people in the building. Get groceries. Things like that.'

'Sounds good.'

Then a marvellous thought came to Terry. 'Would you like me to make chicken for dinner?' she asked eagerly. 'I could try to make that chicken mole you loved so much in Tijuana.'

'No, thanks; don't bother,' Michael said. Then, seeing the disappointment in Terry's face, he added, 'Well, we'll see about it when I get home.'

'When will that be?' Terry asked, trying to sound casual.

'Three or four. No later than four-thirty.'

'Ah,' Terry said, and added a little wistfully, 'Maybe you could give me a call around lunchtime.'

He laughed. 'I would, but we don't have a phone.'

She laughed, too. He kissed her and was gone.

The morning Terry spent unpacking in the new apartment was horrible. The clothes, wrinkled and sand-laden, looked like ghosts of their Tijuana selves, and she could hardly bear to look at them. She had no iron, so she tried steaming the outfits over the bathtub, but this was a disaster. When Michael's best blazer fell into the water, she gave up on the clothes.

It was then that Terry began to notice how quiet everything seemed in Evanston. She could hear cars beneath her window, but no footsteps, no voices, no laughter. And the apartment was strangely still. There were none of the homey noises she always listened for; squeaking cupboards, chirping floorboards. The apartment was too new for that. And no radio or television was playing, because there was no radio or television to play. At first Terry didn't mind the silence so much, and then she began to mind it very much indeed. It was almost as if the apartment were holding its breath, making up its mind and deciding it didn't want her there.

Maybe I'll feel better if I go outside, Terry thought. She got dressed and took the rusty elevator down. The day had turned unpleasantly warm. She wished she had worn a cotton dress instead of jeans, but she did not want to face going up to the empty rooms again and changing. Coming up the front stairs of the building was a neighbour – a young woman with a small, angry-looking baby in her arms. Terry smiled tentatively, but the woman looked at her so coolly that the rush of hello died on Terry's lips. She remembered her wifely boasts to Michael this morning about how she was going to knock on doors, get to know the neighbours. She felt ashamed.

She finally did explore several blocks of the unprepossessing neighbourhood, and she bought a few groceries. She also got a magazine full of household decorating tips and read it, frowning with concentration, in a grimy little park. Whenever the wind blew, she glanced up to make sure there were no twisters above her.

When Terry had finished the last page of the magazine, she could think of nothing else to do, so she went back to the apartment and sat in the square, empty rooms some more. At two o'clock, the doorbell rang. Sunshine returned overwhelmingly. Michael was back! She tore to the door, flung it open. But it was only a UPS man making a delivery. Terry hoped it was the shipment from home – the pots and pans, the radio, the wedding presents, the clothes. That would give her something worthwhile to do – if she hurried, she might even have all the boxes unpacked by the time Michael came home. That ought to impress him. But the UPS man only gave her one small package.

Terry sat on the floor and opened it. It was an album of photographs that her uncle had taken of the wedding. Terry began to cry. Slowly she went through the pictures, each one a poignant assault on her memory. Timmy, in the ridiculous top hat he had insisted on wearing. Her mother, unsmiling in the shadows, looking like the daguerreotype of a pioneer woman a hundred years ago. And her father – hugging Terry as she had left for the honeymoon. She could remember the spongy feel of the tears in his beard. And Michael – how fantastically handsome he looked in his rented morning coat; while she, in her pregnancy wedding dress, looked – Terry felt carefully around for the right word, and finally found it. Plain.

She shrugged, turning over more pages slowly. Minutely she examined every photograph of every guest. They were important people, terribly important now – simply because they had been there at her wedding. Each one of them had taken away one piece of the experience – how the cake had tasted, a certain song the band had played, a piece of news heard over the hors d'oeuvre table, and the wedding would live as long as they did; in a hundred, rich fragments.

The last picture in the album was one of Julie. Terry gasped. It was the most beautiful photograph of Julie that she had ever seen. Julie was standing in a ring of light, her hands clasped tightly in front of her like a little girl, her wavy hair let loose and topped with a circlet of flowers. She looked like a Renaissance portrait in a museum; varnished, rich, warm. Only her face was not warm. It was exquisite but remote.

Coming upon this picture so unexpectedly made Terry flush. Sorrow seemed to steal into the room behind her.

'Why didn't Julie give us a wedding present, Michael?' had been her perplexed, mournful question over and over during the past two weeks. 'I know we haven't seen much of each other lately. I wasn't expecting anything elaborate. But something – anything. I don't understand.' And then always, more sadly still, 'She was the best friend I ever had.'

'Don't think about it,' Michael told her every time. 'Just don't think about it.'

The afternoon was beginning to wear down. The light coming into the apartment was rust-coloured. Terry longed for Michael to come now. She looked hopefully at her watch. Three-forty-five. He should be here any minute. He had said, 'no later than four-thirty.'

But at four-thirty he wasn't home. The sun was low in the sky now. It looked foreign, different than it did setting over the neighbourhood in Los Angeles. Terry began to feel nervous, but she told herself not to get so emotional. She took another walk to the corner shop for more home decorating magazines. She told herself that Michael would be in the apartment when she got back, all excited about his day and wanting to talk.

'Where were you?' he would complain.

'I guess I got so busy the time just slipped by,' she would tell him.

But she came in the door to silence. Michael was not there.

Terry sat on the floor and read the magazines. She would look at a sentence and then at her watch. She was not understanding anything she was reading. It was six now. Six-thirty. At quarter to seven, her hands began to shake as she turned the pages of the magazines. She told herself over and over not to be so silly, but mines of fear began to explode in her head. Michael getting knifed on campus. Michael venturing on to the highway in his car, anxious to get home to her, and an articulated lorry coming the wrong way.

It was seven-thirty now. She was sure, deadly sure, that something was wrong. But what could she do? What could she do? She was far too frightened to weep. Quickly she ran from the apartment. The street looked different at night, completely alien; a street in which any terrible thing seemed not only possible, but probable.

She walked for blocks until she found a pay 'phone. The light inside was very dim. She called Northwestern Registration, Northwestern Information, but no one answered. Each ring made her seem more and more cut off. She wanted to start screaming. She called the campus patrol and asked if there had been any trouble that night. 'Not that we know of,' she was told with some amusement. Not that they knew of! Oh, Michael! Michael, darling!

Her forehead ached. Who else could she call? What names from Northwestern did she know? There was a

professor she and Michael had met at a party. Oh, God –
what was his name? Peters! That was it. No, not Peters,
Peter. No, Pater. Pater. Surely Professor Pater would
remember seeing Michael in class today. Surely Michael
would have gone up to him afterwards and said hello. Surely
he could tell her where Michael was.

Terry pushed the dime in with fingers that shook, called
Information, and got Professor Pater's home number. The
teacher picked up the 'phone himself. Terry sobbed out her
story.

Yes, Professor Pater said confusedly, after a pause; he did
remember meeting her and Michael at the party – but no, he
was afraid he couldn't remember if Michael had been in
class today. He had four hundred students, you see. But he
was terribly sorry. He hoped that everything would be all
right. Terry hung up the 'phone. She had no more dimes.

Slowly she left the booth and crept, whimpering, back
down the six blocks to the apartment. She would wait till
the morning to tell Michael's mother that her son was dead.
She opened the apartment door and was met by a blaze of
lights.

'Michael!' she shrieked, running sobbing into his arms.

'Where were you?' he asked, annoyed. 'I would at least
have thought that you'd be here to meet me on our first
night.'

Terry backed away from him, speechless. 'Where was *I*?
Where were *you*?' she hollered at last. 'You said four-thirty
at the latest! It's almost nine!'

'Sorry,' he said. One eyebrow was raised in a look Terry
had never seen on him before. 'I met some guys from high
school, and we went out for a few drinks. I didn't know
you'd get so upset about it.'

Terry couldn't hold herself back. She found herself
screaming out terrible things, while Michael looked silently
on as though she were a lunatic. But when he heard how she
had called Professor Pater on the telephone, he started

screaming back. It was their first fight, and they didn't make it up till nearly dawn.

By the second month of their marriage, Terry and Michael had begun to fight about money.

'I can't understand you,' Michael would tell her tightly when Terry came home with a tiny potted violet or a new record or a framed poster for the living room wall. 'Here I am, studying my ass off, waiting on tables at weekends so we can buy groceries; your parents have mortgaged their house so we can live in this apartment, and you spend your whole time buying goddammed knickknacks.'

For a few weeks Terry reformed and stuck to essentials; but then one afternoon she was passing by Marshall Fields and encountered some 'Aramis' for men. It smelled so delicious that she couldn't resist buying a tiny bottle for Michael. When he unwrapped it that afternoon, he didn't say anything. He stood up, put on his coat, made Terry put on hers, walked with her in silence back to the store and asked to see the general manager.

'I am returning this cologne,' he told him. 'And I never want you to sell my wife anything again.'

The next morning, Terry got a job. She worked as a saleslady in the maternity shop of a nearby shopping mall. It was not bad work. Terry discovered that she had some talent for the job, and she enjoyed being around other young mothers-to-be. But at the same time, working in the shop made her a little wistful. It was hard seeing all the young husbands coming in to help their wives choose dresses, so interested and so proud.

On her lunch hour, Terry usually wandered through thrift shops and second-hand stores, trying to find furniture for the apartment. Michael was always complaining about how bare it looked. Terry grew more and more depressed. Nothing she saw was remotely what she wanted – nothing was pretty or delicate enough. Then one day she happened to pass by an elegant antique shop. In the window was a tiny French loveseat covered in pale cream satin with tiny blue forget-me-nots hand-embroidered on the fabric. Terry gasped.

That's it! she thought joyfully. That's what I'm going to buy! Every young couple needs one good antique.

It was the tiny kick striking inside Terry's slightly swollen belly that brought her crashing to earth. She would buy it? An eighteenth-century loveseat? Why, she didn't even have enough money to buy a baby crib. Shame ran across Terry's face in a red rush. She must be losing her mind. She saw a panicked vision of their apartment, with its inventory of one bed, one formica breakfast table, three unmatched chairs, a clock radio, and the curtains with the tomatoes on them. Terry sat down on the kerb and began to cry. Then she got up, walked into the first junk shop she could find, and bought the cheapest, ugliest, most service-able couch they had to offer.

The apartment was furnished within a week.

As the months passed, Terry began to suffer a sharp pain in her groin. Her obstetrician said it was nothing serious, but advised her to stay off her feet as much as possible. Terry was sorry to have to leave her job at the maternity shop, but there was no choice.

She found staying at home all day terribly dull. But as time went on, she got quite adept at inventing all kinds of tricks to make the days pass. When she was vacuuming with the asthmatic electric broom she and Michael had bought at a garage sale, she would tell herself that if she didn't get up every bit of lint from the carpet, the detective watching through the keyhole was going to burst in and throw her in jail. Or, if she didn't manage to clean every smidgen of burnt spaghetti sauce from the pan, Michael was going to fail his exams. So she vacuumed and scrubbed like a fiend. Cleaning the windows became the high point of her day once she convinced herself that she was going for the world's speed record. Could she shave five seconds off last week's time? Ready, set, go! She did it! Hearing the cheers of an imaginary audience, she recorded her time in a little notebook. Doing the laundry became a positive pleasure, once she had developed a personal relationship with all the clothes. 'Now what seems to be the problem this week?' she would ask Michael's plaid shirt soothingly. 'A little grease on the pocket? Nothing to worry about – we'll soon take care of that.'

Only once did Michael catch her in the act, singing to the silverware. Blushingly, Terry tried to explain about her little games, but he didn't understand. 'You're a head case,' he told her, only half laughing.

'Exactly,' she responded, a little hurt. 'Doing a good job at anything always starts with the mind.'

Michael's hours seemed to grow later and later. Sometimes he wouldn't get home from the library or from drinks with his friends until ten at night, and he would come home to find Terry, weepy and sullen, in bed with the covers pulled up belligerently.

'You could at least have let me know!' she would emerge long enough to say. 'I've been alone all day, and you promised we could go to a movie tonight.'

'Your problem is that you don't have any friends,' he would tell her. And the bedclothes would be flounced back up.

It seemed to Terry that, after the rise and fall of her friendship with Julie, she just didn't have the heart to make another friend. She had made a few unenthusiastic over-tures to a few of the women in the apartment building, but they hadn't really worked out. Eileen Flanagan was on the fifth floor, and was also seventeen. Terry thought that because Eileen was so pretty, she could at least tell her about new ways of doing her hair, or give her tips about

95

wearing make-up. But Eileen turned out to be hideously dull. She was married to a cesspool cleaner with a severe psoriasis condition, and Eileen was always out shopping for new lotions that might cure it.

Jean Kew lived on Terry's floor. She was very tidy and timid-looking, but at least she had a sense of humour, as Terry discovered the day she and Jean were carrying their rubbish to the basement and a mouse ran amok. But on further acquaintance, Terry discovered that all Jean thought and talked about was the month she and her husband Stan had spent in Spain, two years before. Her whole living room was decorated with posters of bullfights, artfully positioned over the peeling paint, and with little dolls in mantillas standing on the coffee table and the bureau. It made Terry very sad to see them.

Sometimes, when she was in the supermarket or walking in the park, Terry would see a tiny girl with long waving yellow hair, and her heart would freeze. She would have to stand still for a moment until it returned to normal. Once or twice she wrote to Julie, long, emotional letters, but when she read them over, she tore them up. Somehow it came out in the letters that she was feeling sorry for herself and unhappy about her life – and she wasn't; she absolutely wasn't. She knew she was the luckiest person in the world.

Sometimes Terry walked around the campus of North-western, but these wanderings often left her feeling a little depressed. She looked shyly at the casually-dressed girls carrying their notebooks, remembering how she had always loved the day-before-school trip to the stationer's. Then, 'What have these girls got?' she would think fiercely. 'Just their silly classes and books. I've got a husband. I've got a baby coming.' But there was one flaw in her argument. In a few years these girls would be out of college, working at important careers, and then they too would have husbands and babies of their own. But not my husband, Terry would quickly tell herself. Not my baby.

She had one very bad afternoon. Walking through the quadrangle on a hot day, she passed by a classroom where an English lesson was in progress. The window was open, and she could hear the teacher asking his freshman class in exasperation, 'Can't *anyone* translate 'Honi soit qui mal y pense'?' There was a sheepish silence. Terry stuck her head in the window, answered, 'Shame to him who thinks ill of it,' and ran away. She cried on the walk home.

One day she stopped for ice cream in the Mall, and a young man sat down beside her at the wrought-iron table. Terry was a little nervous, but what could possibly happen, she argued to herself, with all these people around? The boy talked to her very pleasantly. He didn't know she was married, because Terry wasn't wearing her wedding ring. It had become too tight on her finger lately, and she had taken it off. She and the boy joked and laughed. But when he got around to asking her if she'd like to see a movie that night, she told him she was sorry, but she was married.

The encounter pleased Terry. It was nice to find that someone still thought she was attractive. On the way home that afternoon, she took out the ten dollars that her mother had sent her the week before and bought herself a sexy new blouse.

It was their six-month anniversary. Terry sat on the windowseat in the sunset waiting for Michael to come home. The baby kicked contentedly in her stomach. Terry smiled down and stroked it with little butterfly touches. Right from the beginning she wanted it to get the idea that it was loved.

By the door, flamboyantly wrapped, was the pigskin satchel she had bought Michael for the anniversary. For weeks, ever since she had seen it in the window of the college store, Terry had babysat every Wednesday and Thursday afternoon to earn the money to buy it. It had been

97

hard keeping the secret from Michael, but she had managed, and now he was going to be most wonderfully surprised and pleased. Terry knew how it had embarrassed him to have to carry his books around in his arms like a high-schooler, just because they couldn't afford a nice briefcase.

And there on the table was the ice-cream cake she had ordered from Baskin Robbins that afternoon. 'We love you – Terry and?' it said in blue icing. The girl at the store had been very puzzled over the message until she had seen Terry's big stomach, and then she had laughed and laughed. Terry smiled to think about it. Yes; the people around here were definitely getting friendlier.

Then Terry looked more closely at the cake and frowned. The icing was starting to look a little melted. Sighing, she put it back in the box, then returned it to the freezer. This was the second time. She looked at her watch again. Michael had promised he would be back at six, and here it was, seven fifteen. By quarter past eight, the cake had been in and out of the freezer four times, and Terry was fuming. It's like some horrible old movie, she thought furiously – the poor pregnant wife waiting at home deserted, while the husband is out – doing what? Those old movies offered her plenty of answers. Terry started to cry, with the combined tears of Judy Holliday, Margaret Sullavan and Olivia de Havilland. It just wasn't fair, she stormed. She hated this place. She hated Michael. She hated marriage.

And then she heard his key in the lock. Terry raced to the freezer, bringing out the cake for the fifth time, and putting a wavery smile on her face. She was prepared to go either way. If Michael had remembered their anniversary, had brought her flowers or a card, she would forgive all; but if he had forgotten, she vowed she would start a scene that Judy Holliday, Margaret Sullavan and Olivia de Havilland couldn't touch.

But Michael hadn't forgotten. He came in the door, smiling, and after he opened his present, which he said he loved, he gave Terry a sweet kiss.

'Happy anniversary to you, too, beautiful wife!' he said, and drawing a package from his pocket, he gave it to Terry. She snatched at it with an eager gasp. Clumsily she tore the wrappings off. Inside was a tiny golden pin, shaped like a bee.

'It's beautiful!' she whispered. She had not, until this moment, known how desperately she wanted a gold pin shaped like a bee.

'One of the women in my class had one,' he told her, 'and I asked her where she got it. It came from a catalogue.'

Proudly Terry pinned the bee to her collar. How funny life was, she thought. Ten minutes ago she had been so wretched because Michael was late, and now she was utterly content because of her bee. But neither emotion quite cancelled the other out. The lateness and the bee were juxtaposed. She guessed they always were. It was hard to get used to the idea that marriage wasn't really like in the movies at all. It wasn't as purely good and it wasn't as purely bad. It was – middling. That was what real life was, she decided – middling. Terry felt very grown-up, even a little bit old, coming to that conclusion.

Three days before Christmas, Michael told Terry that he wanted to have a few friends over for drinks. It was their first party, and Terry was very excited. She did much poring through magazines to see what canapés the perfect wives were serving these days, and spent hours deciding what she was going to wear. Finally she let out the seams of her long green skirt and tried it with her new white blouse. It looked fine. There was no way anyone could see the opened zipper or the two safety pins holding the skirt together. The morning of the event she was up at six o'clock, muttering happily to Michael about how much there was left to do.

But the cocktail party was a disappointment. After having heard so much about Michael's friends, Terry was greatly excited about meeting them and was rather taken aback by how blasé they seemed in return. Perhaps, she thought, it was because they had not heard quite so much about her.

Terry had the opportunity, that evening, of meeting the young woman who had given Michael the idea for the bee pin. Her name was Helen. She was wearing a rose-coloured kaftan and golden sandals. Terry kept wondering how Helen had made it through the snow in those shoes. Perhaps she had come in ugly boots and stored them outside in the hall. Or perhaps she had – unheard of in poverty-infested college circles – taken a taxi. She looked quite wealthy. Helen had a sharply trimmed helmet of golden hair, and Terry tried hard not to think of the thousand ships.

Terry was a vigorous, if not downright ostentatious, hostess, refilling drinks and emptying ashtrays. It bothered her slightly that Michael did not help; he accepted the wine and the cigarettes she offered, like a guest among guests. Well, what did she expect? Terry asked herself angrily. Michael to stand with his arm around her, talking proudly about the little woman? She had been watching too many of those movies again.

As the evening went on, Terry saw more and more clearly that she was in no way a part of it. All her preparations were unnoticed. The guests ate the cheese straws without complaint and without praise. Only Helen kept protesting how delicious everything was. Terry found she was growing very tense. It bothered her to hear Michael and his friends arguing so spiritedly about technical questions from their courses. It shamed her that she could not follow what they were saying, even though she tried. In fact she tried so hard her teeth were gritted. And it was a surprise, the way Michael was listening with real attention and respect to everything Helen was saying. Terry reflected that going to the Mall every day didn't give her a whole lot to talk to him about.

'My goodness, you're efficient! I'm getting exhausted just

100

watching you!' Helen smiled at her, watching Terry scuttle grimly to the kitchen with a quartet of dirty ashtrays.

'I'm getting exhausted just watching you!' Terry mimicked Helen to Michael in bed that evening. 'Well, why couldn't she have helped me?' She had meant to sound merely gay, but Michael did not miss the edge in her voice.

Something in his sigh was like nails shrieking across a blackboard.

But there was one thing in Terry's life that was unquestionably perfect. That was waiting for the baby. It was strange, Terry reflected one evening, sitting on the wooden windowseat with one arm curled protectively around her stomach. When we first got married, I always thought about the baby as being Michael's and mine – but now I want it to be just mine.

Terry made all kinds of little sneaky plans to ensure that this would happen. She would breastfeed, so that there would be bonding. She would make Michael do the disciplining, and she would do the comforting. She would say 'Mama' a hundred times a day to the baby so that that would be its first word. She would never say 'Daddy'. She would arrange the baby's schedule so that it would be asleep when Michael came home.

As she entered her ninth month of pregnancy, Terry lived constantly within the thought of the baby. The housework forgotten, she would spend her days on the windowseat, watching and evaluating the world that her baby was coming into. And, crazily, whenever the 'phone rang, she half expected it to be the baby calling.

It was going to be a boy. He would be sensitive and manly. He would never answer back. There would be none of the soul-stabbing fights that Terry had had with her own mother. Or with Michael. He would hold her arm over the icy patches in the road. And his name would be Christopher Robin. When she read him the Pooh books, she would say,

'See – they're all about you,' and he would love that. And Christopher would look not like Michael but like Terry's own father. Exactly like him. And when he grew up, he would have a red beard, too.

Terry could see, as it got closer to her due date, that Michael was also getting excited about the baby. He took pre-natal classes so that he could be there at the delivery, he felt the rapid little kicks in Terry's stomach each evening; and when Terry peeked at a letter he had written to his folks, she had to smile to see how proudly he spoke of his 'coming first-born.' She was touched by Michael's interest, but it did not change things. Fair was fair. Michael had college. Michael had friends. Michael had the upper hand in everything. But the baby was hers.

Michael's first semester grades came in the mail one morning when he was out. Terry, the expert on old movies, knew exactly what to do – but steaming letters open over tea-kettles is a messier business than Technicolor would have one believe. Still, she managed to open the envelope at last.

Michael had got all C's.

Terry stared at the paper in stunned shame.

At six that evening, Michael called to say he would be working late at the library. Terry did not mention the report card. She didn't feel too well, so she defrosted a Swanson Mexican dinner, ate it, then went to bed. At ten o'clock, she awakened with stomach cramps. Blast those beans, she thought, and tried to go back to sleep. At eleven o'clock, she was composing a letter, threatening to sue Swansons. At midnight, it began to occur to her that the pains might not be food poisoning after all.

Terry panicked – for twenty minutes she sat on the edge of the bed, trying to decide what to do. Should she call Michael or not? She could have him paged at the library – but if it turned out to be a false alarm, she knew how annoyed he would be. On the other hand, if it was the baby coming and he missed being at the hospital because she didn't call, he would be even madder. Finally, Terry hit on the perfect plan – she would take a taxi to the hospital and ask to be examined. If it was only food poisoning, she would creep home and never let Michael know what a fool she had been. But if it was the baby, she would call Michael from the hospital and tell him to come over.

Terry never got a chance to call Michael. She barely had time to call the taxi. For forty-five minutes later, Christopher Robin Spenser was born.

Terry would never forget, as long as she lived, the sensation of the baby's head being pulled like a champagne cork from her, or the first sight of that scarlet and white baby, as triumphant and emblematic as a waving flag. And when she held Christopher in her arms for the first time, she knew that her purpose had been found; that the days of aimlessness had come to an end.

The two days Terry spent in the hospital were utter euphoria. Her parents had never been able to afford to send her to summer camp as a child, but this hospital stay was everything Terry had imagined summer camp to be. Every hour, there was something new and pleasant to do. Meals to be eaten – although they were disappointing, it was fun being served on a tray – presents from home to open, Michael's friends to receive, bed baths to take, and the baby to feed and admire.

She was given a room-mate, a black girl called Jeanette who had just had her second baby girl. Jeanette wasn't very happy about it, and Terry felt sorry for her. No one had sent Jeanette or baby Sarah any flowers or gifts, so Terry shared those she and Christopher received.

She was touched by how many people sent things. Her grandmother sent flowers and also Helen, Michael's beautiful friend. Michael's parents sent a card which, if not exactly ecstatic, was friendly; and Dena, the nun, sent a St

Christopher medal. Terry was thrilled by the layette of sweaters and booties her own mother had knitted, and by the tiny model train her father enclosed, 'to start Christopher off on the right track'. But the gift which touched Terry the most was the enormous shipment that arrived from her brother. Timmy was part-owner of a sports goods store now, and he must have sent everything in their winter stock. There were ice skates in every size, hockey sticks, helmets, footballs and boots. Terry cried for fifteen minutes when that gift came.

There was no present from Julie. Of course not. She had not been told about the birth. 'Why bother?' Michael had asked, when Terry suggested that she send a letter. 'She won't care.' But it was odd. Nearly every time Terry held Christopher in her arms, she found herself thinking of Julie and the first time that she had ever seen her. She had felt almost the same way then as she did now – thrilled by the tininess of the beloved, and overcome with the desire to protect it.

Michael was delighted with his son. He came to the hospital whenever he got off from class, and sat in the hard wooden chair doing homework. Terry was always pleased to see him, but it was a little jarring. Michael brought in the real world, with all of its tedious problems. Terry had forgotten to pay the 'phone bill, it seemed, so their line had been disconnected. And, in her final frantic rush to the hospital, she had left a boiling teakettle on the stove, nearly blowing up the apartment. But Terry did not get upset or even feel guilty as she would have done a month before.

Looking down at Christopher sucking with such happy drunkenness at her breast, she only felt sorry that Michael had to have such unhappy things on his mind.

Terry was sorry when the time came to leave the hospital. After all, the happiest hours of her life had been spent there. But she was also glad to be starting real life with Christopher at last.

When the taxi let them off at their apartment building, Michael, thinking of Terry's stitches, wanted to carry Christopher. But Terry wouldn't give the baby up to him. She carried Christopher up the four flights herself.

Michael had tried hard to get the apartment ready for the home-coming. The second-hand crib had come, and he had put on all the sheets (inside out) and pushed it against a wall (the wrong one). He had even gone out and bought a horrible little mobile. A week's worth of dirty dishes was piled neatly in the sink so that it wouldn't be an eyesore, and the dirty laundry was tidily folded in the hamper.

Terry fed the baby, put him in the crib and covered him up. It was amazing how naturally it all came to her. Then she cleaned up a little of the mess. Michael watched her.

'I've got a piece of news,' he said suddenly. 'I ran into Professor Pater in the hall yesterday. We got talking, and he told me about a job opening up this summer. His brother's starting an insurance firm in the area, and they need a dogsbody. Pater says medical jobs for the summer are just about impossible to get, and he thinks I should take this.' Michael shrugged. 'I don't know. It would probably make more sense to take some summer courses, but the money would sure help,' he added, a little self-consciously, 'now that we have new responsibilities.'

Terry was only half listening. She was looking around the apartment, pretending she was Christopher, and seeing everything with his eyes. It was awesome to think that his first subconscious memories would be created here. The ceiling was cracked overhead. That was ugly to a grown-up, but curiously alive and interesting when you were a baby on the floor. And the block of beige curtains was definitely soothing. Oh, yes, how glad she was to have got rid of the tomato curtains. Something that ugly might have warped Christopher's personality forever.

'Of course you'll take the job,' she said cheerily to Michael. 'We need the money, and you can't insult

Professor Pater. Besides, if it goes well, you can work there every summer. Maybe they'll even offer you a position when you graduate.'

And the crib looked like the gates of a fairy-tale castle, looming, forbidding, yet ready to be conquered.

Michael blinked. 'What?' he asked with a laugh. 'Terry are you listening? This is an *insurance* firm I'm talking about. I'm going to be a doctor. Remember?'

Terry hummed a little song. Christopher seemed to like it, so she hummed it again. 'I remember,' she said, 'but things do change, you know. And they say it's good to keep your options open.'

'But I don't want them open,' Michael said. His voice was becoming tight.

Terry loosened Christopher's nappy, for fear it was imparing his circulation. 'I think it would be kind of nice, your being in insurance,' she said musingly. 'You'd get home at a decent hour. We could buy a nice house in the area, and Christopher could play in the backyard. Wouldn't you like that, Christopher?' she cried, tickling his kicking feet. 'Chasing your own squirrels in your own backyard?'

Michael shut his eyes for a moment. 'Listen, Terry,' he said heavily. 'I don't want to be stuck here. That was never the plan. The plan was, and remains, that when I finish Med. School we're moving to New York and I'm practising there.'

'All right,' Terry said. 'Forget it. Be anything you want to be. I don't care.' Then she thought of the C's on the report card, and added more gently, 'But things do change, you know. That was the only point I was trying to make. Just don't be so rigid. We'll see what happens, when it happens, We'll wait and see.'

Michael tried not to be so rigid. He made little clucking sounds and clapped his hands. 'Come on, Chris,' he said. 'Smile for Daddy.'

Terry was silent a moment. 'Do you think you could

manage not to call him Chris?' she asked politely.
'Christopher is his name.'

Julie got Terry's letter about the baby. 'He reminds me of
you,' Terry had added in a tiny rushed postcript. Julie
stared at the photograph of the wrinkled little face and tried
to figure this out.

She didn't know what she was supposed to do with the
picture. She started to throw it out, but then on an impulse
she picked it up and stuck it on the edge of her mirror.

When the boy came over that night, he noticed it. 'Who's
the kid?' he asked.

'He's mine,' Julie told him. 'Don't you think he looks
just like me?'

'We two form a multitude.'

Terry had loved that expression from the time she first
heard it, but it was not until Christopher was born that she
realized it was true. Together she and the baby were even
more than a multitude – for multitudes implied diversity.
Together they were a world. Her half of it was large and
faltering and over-anxious; his half was compact, complete
and sure. But this lopsided world was flourishing.

Christopher was not what is generally known as a good
baby. He did not sleep when he was supposed to, he would
not get on the proper feeding schedule, and his constant
dramatic crying considerably unnerved Michael and the rest
of the apartment building dwellers. But Terry knew there
was nothing wrong with her son.

'He had an unsettling experience this evening,' she would
explain, setting out Michael's plate of canned spaghetti. It
was all she had time to cook these days; canned foods and
TV dinners. 'He heard that man in the apartment upstairs
yelling at the lady he's living with.'

Or she might say, 'He's a little mad at me tonight because
I tried to make him wear blue booties with his green pants.

I'm afraid he's getting to be rather a dandy.' Michael would shake his head and smile nervously. He wasn't sure whether Terry believed these things she was saying or not.

Terry believed them. By the time the baby was one-and-a-half months old, she had evolved a whole personality for him. What sort of music he liked, what sort of women, what sort of weather. And she carried on long conversations with him about these matters.

She also held Christopher a great deal. Sometimes she would just sit on the windowsill, the room a wreck behind her, and just hold him for an hour. They watched the sun set together every day. Terry was convinced that there were certain shades of gold and rose Christopher preferred. 'He's going to be an artist when he grows up,' she would tell Michael proudly. Other days he was going to be a musician, or an architect, or a dancer. But never, for some reason, a doctor.

And the ritual of being a mother – the two a.m. feedings, the slag heap of laundry and nappies, the eternally changing strategies to keep Christopher from crying, or getting him to go to sleep – these did not really bother Terry, did not make her feel in any way diminished. On the contrary, there was a euphoria about her constant exhaustion. She grew to love the routine, the almost religious dedication of every day to the small pink idol.

But the nicest part of every day was the afternoon walk. Rainy or sunny, she pushed Christopher in his pram that she named 'The Blue Rolls-Royce', along the little towpath behind the apartment building. Michael expressed concern at its isolation, but Terry refused to be worried. She knew that nothing bad was going to happen to herself or to Christopher. The seasons passed gaily or gravely; the leaves and the colours came and changed. Walking the same path at the same time every day gave the event importance. It was a heavy golden thread in the frail, shifting fabric of daily life.

That summer was the most beautiful one Terry had ever

seen. Christopher delighted in the sunbeams, the shifting trees. And his face, pale like Michael's, looked sweet and sad, sweet and sad, according to whether there was sun or shadow overhead.

As time went on, Terry found she did not like it when other people tried to climb over the gate into the world she and her son had made together. She grew to hate any interference, any suggestions, any involvement whatsoever. She didn't like it when strangers stopped her on the street to chat to Christopher. She liked it even less when they thought he was a little girl. She resented it terribly when the woman upstairs said that Christopher's cap would chafe his neck and ought to be loosened. She was blue all afternoon, when Christopher gave his biggest smile to the postman. She almost hit Michael the night he said Christopher was spoiled. And the day she got a four-page letter from her mother, telling her exactly how her grandson should be raised, Terry went mad. She hurled the letter in the wastepaper basket and jumped up and down on it until it was dead. She hated everything, everything that even hinted that Christopher belonged to the wide world and not exclusively to her.

The third of August was Michael's birthday. In the evening, Terry sat on the sofa with Christopher, waiting for Michael to come home from his summer job at the insurance firm. There was no present waiting for him, for she had simply not had the time to go to the Mall and look for one. But Michael would understand.

At least there was a cake on the table. She had meant to bake one from scratch, but there had been no time for that either. The square chocolate Pepperidge Farm cake looked a little strange sitting on the round serving dish that Uncle Julian had given them for a wedding present, but she was sure Michael wouldn't even notice.

She stroked Christopher's cool little head and told him three fairy stories in a row. Behind her, the apartment was very messy and not terribly clean, but she did not have the interest or energy to do anything about it. She only wanted to sit with her living baby on her lap, and feel his starfish hands crawl over her face.

At eight o'clock, Terry and Christopher both began to grow sleepy. Terry didn't think they could wait up for Michael any longer. She started to lay Christopher down in his crib, but he was too sweet to give up, so she took him into the bed with her and curled up around him like a peach around a stone. We two form a multitude, she thought sleepily.

When she heard Michael's key jarring in the lock at half-past nine, she awoke with a startled, breathless jerk. And Christopher began to scream.

On a bright July evening soon after Michael's graduation from Northwestern, the Spensers moved into their newly rented house, located in a cheerful suburb of Evanston.

Waking up the following morning, Terry felt the very same childish panic that she had felt four years before, when she had awakened after the honeymoon. Only this time she had unpacked the coffee mugs. Michael wanted to make a favourable impression, his first morning at work, so he left the house early for the insurance firm. Terry watched through the uncurtained dining-room window as he left. He looked very young, stepping confidently down the un-planted garden path, as if he were play-acting the part of head of the family. He had told Terry that his not being able to get into Medical School was all for the best – and that if he had become a doctor, they wouldn't have been able to afford to live in a house like this for another six years.

The sound of sudden shrieking turned Terry from the window. Christopher came racing out of his room in a panic. She had laid him asleep in his new bedroom last night, and he had awakened to find the familiar furniture swathed in what he thought were mouldering shrouds.

110

The neighbours came by all that morning bringing frosted cakes, in the best friendly Midwestern tradition. But Terry, distracted by arranging the furniture, seeing that the telephone man didn't soil the rug with his dirty tools, and keeping Christopher from putting his hand in the garbage disposal, was a little brusque in her thanks. She felt the neighbours' all-absorbing eyes. Christopher is spoiled, she thought. And I am in a housedress with a dirty collar.

Even though she had wanted it more than anything, for a moment Terry was sorry they had moved. I will never get along with these women, she thought in exasperation. I will never feel comfortable in a place where all the houses look the same. I will never buy a station wagon. I willl never take up tennis. And I will definitely never grow roses.

But by mid-afternoon she was happier – for Christopher had made up his mind that the new house was Paradise. Down in the basement, he told his mother excitedly, he had found Robin Hood's lair. And when Terry watched him run outside to play, a memory she hadn't thought of in many years came to her. It was the morning she and her family had moved into the new house in Santa Monica. She had been three years old – just Christopher's age. She remembered the wild joy of sitting in the empty bedroom, decorating it in hundreds of imaginary frilly ways, and being absolutely furious when her mother slapped her for finding the painter's bucket and trying to help him with the green trim. Terry had to laugh. Poor Mama, she thought wryly. I can see why she was so grumpy sometimes.

As the weeks went on, Terry found that she was thinking of her mother a lot. When she walked around the Mall, choosing new towels or stainless steel, she would see other young wives towing their captive mothers along, and she would grow wistful. She would occasionally pretend that her own mother was beside her, agreeing enthusiastically with the slipcovers she was choosing.

I wish we'd been closer, Terry thought. Whose fault was it that we weren't? Mine, mostly, she admitted to herself. I was so busy wishing Mama was glamorous like Julie's mother that I never realized all she had in her. And she remembered a day when she was five years old – when she had told her mother that Mrs Adams was the most beautiful mother she had ever seen. How that must have hurt Mama, Terry thought. I'm so sorry I did that.

Impulsively, she sat down and wrote her mother a note. '*Come for a visit,*' she said. '*What about September 15? Not Daddy – just you. We'll choose slipcovers.*'

The telephone rang, and Terry picked it up. It was her father. He said the accident had been very sudden, and that Terry's mother hadn't suffered at all.

Terry couldn't get out of bed for three days. Michael was sympathetic at first. Then, when Terry wasn't up to cooking him dinner for the fourth night in a row, he snapped at her to grow up. 'Your mother hadn't been part of your life in years!' he reminded her.

Terry picked up the vase on her bedside table and threw it at his head. Then she locked herself in the bedroom and would not come out. She only opened the door to Christopher. She would hold him in her arms on the bed, even though she knew he was not enjoying it. 'We're going to be close,' she would murmur. 'We're going to be part of each other's lives forever.'

It was a sickly afternoon in late December. Terry had brought all the wrong clothes. The fog which had hung over Los Angeles all morning like tacky fake snow on Christmas trees, had finally lifted. Terry walked down Santa Monica Boulevard, too warm in her wool dress. Great, purposeless misery vibrated within her. As she passed the Salvation Army stands, her heart wailed in contrapuntal rhythm to the carols the officers were singing.

Christopher, four years old, tugged, puzzled, on her hand. 'Mama, is this really the place where you grew up?'

'Yes,' she said. 'But it was pretty then.'

They passed a supermarket. Taped to one window was a poster of a large family enjoying themselves in a firelit room. 'Have an old-fashioned Christmas,' the caption commanded.

'When I was little, there were no stores on this street,' Terry told Christopher. 'Only pretty little bungalows.' Christopher looked around, scowling. Clearly he didn't believe her.

They walked back to the car park and got into the Mustang Terry had rented for this week-long trip. Michael had told her she was mad, taking Christopher off to California like this. Perhaps she was. It was only the second day, and already the little boy was missing his tricycle and Artie next door. But Terry had wanted him with her.

They drove. The fog was beginning to return. Within it, the small red Mustang looked like a wet flame. The traffic was slow and unsure.

When Terry came upon the cemetery, it was a shock. A wrong turning in the fog. But once she saw it, she knew she must go inside. Apprehensively, she looked over at Christopher, but he was unaware of where they were. He was gazing eagerly out the window, pressing his nose against it, and laughing at some silent joke he had with the fog.

Terry had heard all the stories about little children scarred for life because they had been introduced to death too soon. But a cemetery wasn't death, she thought. She would tell Christopher that it was only a pretty garden.

She parked the car. She stepped out on to the neatly cut grass, grateful that there was nothing spooky, nothing to fear. Christopher hopped out, his face bright. He loved flowers. Even through the fog they glowed on the graves and he ran towards them. Terry hushed him softly, like the fading echo of his footsteps.

She found her mother's grave after a long search. It was neatly tended, as were all the other graves, unassuming, the headstone Protestant in its regularity and conventional inscription.

Terry felt cold inside. No! she wanted to shout. Mama wasn't like that; so chilly, so worn. Mama was wonderful. And so alive. Mama is alive! she wanted to cry. But she couldn't.

'Mama! Mama!' Terry cried in anguished silence; but only silence answered her.

Christopher came up, dewy and sweet in the fog. Seeing his mother staring down at the grave, he bent and began tracing the inscription. Terry stopped him. He smiled up at her.

'Ice cream?' he asked.

'Ice cream,' she answered. She took his miniature hand and they walked away from the grave. She was terribly glad that he would not be scarred – that he was too young to know what death was. And yet, as they got back to their fiery red Mustang, Terry wanted to weep. Because he was too young to know.

They were having dinner at the home of Serge Carter, Michael's most important client. Terry, in her best black dress, was sitting on the plastic-covered crushed velvet sofa, staring dumbly down at the platter of hors d'oeuvres Lynn Carter was offering. It depressed her that she knew from exactly which grocery store counter magazine Lynn had got the recipe. She knew because she had made it herself last week, when the Gethers had come to dinner. The Carters this week, the Gethers last week, the Wildes next week. 'We don't need all these people,' she would cry. 'Why can't we be alone just once, just you and me and Christopher?'

'Because of business, Terry,' Michael would tell her tightly. 'It has to be done for business.'

Serge Carter was telling another story of how he had got the best of a Jew in a deal. Terry fantasized about going over and kicking him very hard in the crotch. Lynn was offering another miniature quiche. Terry took it. She might as well add overweight to the rest of her miseries. Michael was laughing at Serge's story in that fawning way Terry hated. Good for business, she kept saying dully to herself.

She looked longingly at the telephone. She had called home twice already – could she get away with it a third time? Her excuse was that she was checking up on the new babysitter – the truth was that she called because hearing Christopher's gay, free little voice in the background made her feel sane again.

Serge Carter started another story – this one was about a rich nigger whose house was burned down by the boys – and the kicker was, he had no insurance. Terry excused herself politely and went into the bathroom. It was wall-papered in shiny foil, and on the floor was a hooked rug, shaped like an owl. Lynn had made it. Terry sat on the toilet seat – it was adorned with a smaller owl – and she began to sob.

It was a hot spring day. The canopies of the small Evanston stores blew brightly in the wind, and the trees rustled with a kind of languid joy. Terry and Christopher were in the large toyshop on Main Street. Next week Christopher would be graduating from kindergarten, and they were here to pick out his present. Of course, Christopher wasn't to know that that was what they were doing. Terry would simply see what he most liked and then secretly come back the next day and buy it.

Terry smiled down at her son, as he dashed from one counter to the next, his face quick with enjoyment. What a beautiful little boy he was. A golden child. Where, oh where, had he come from? she wondered. Christopher made many thrilling discoveries along the aisles, but it was only when he found the plush giraffe that appreciation turned into need.

He ran to his mother with the giraffe and thrust it into her hands. Terry pulled a string in its back to make it talk, and Christopher laughed till he was breathless at its ridiculous voice.

'Make it say something for you, Mama!' he pleaded, and Terry pulled the string again.

'When I get a sore throat, it really hurts!' Giraffe confided.

'I'm sorry to hear that,' Terry told it gravely. 'Someone ought to knit you a nice warm scarf.'

Christopher listened to the conversation in delight.

'Would you like to come home with us, Giraffe?' Terry asked.

'I like you,' Giraffe answered.

'He does want to come!' Christopher was awed.

Terry smiled idiotically down at her son, forgetting all plans to save the present as a surprise. 'OK,' she said. 'Happy graduation.'

While Terry paid for the toy, Christopher carried Giraffe over to the enormous papier-mâché tree in the centre of the toyshop. If a certain little spigot was pulled the right way, a stream of lemonade gushed miraculously forth. He was on his fourth paper cupful when Terry joined him. They sat together on the bench under the fairy-tale tree, and talked about the grand future they and Giraffe would have together.

'Terry! Terry Garvey! I don't believe it!'

Terry looked up.

It was Eunice Blackinstock from high school, looking astonishingly the same after all these years. She wore the same coil of hair on her neck, she had the same blue plastic glasses. Even her teeth had still never been straightened.

For a moment, seeing Eunice like this seemed to be the most natural thing in the world – it was as if they were really still back in the days of tenth grade, as if Michael and

Christopher were just a dream in the future, and the only reality was this week's chemistry quiz.

'It's wonderful to see you,' Terry said warmly. 'Sit right down and tell me what's been happening in the past hundred years.'

Actually, the two of them had never been close friends. They had not really been friends at all. Eunice had been Julie's lab partner, and there had always been a slight rivalry between her and Terry for Julie's attention. A slight one, only, because Eunice had never stood a chance.

But none of that mattered anymore.

'Oh, nothing much is going on in my life,' Eunice admitted pleasantly. 'I'm a computer technician.'

'You always were good at maths,' Terry was pleased to remember. 'Do you live nearby?'

'No – I stayed in California. I'm just here for a few days on business. Do *you* live here, Terry?' she asked after a beat, looking around at the small Main Street in some surprise.

'Yes,' Terry said, flushing slightly – she did not know why. 'My husband and I are very happy here.'

Eunice nodded. 'Yes, I remember hearing you got married. Do you work, as well? Weren't you going to be a teacher or something?'

Terry smiled 'Actually, I *have* started a local daycare centre. I don't suppose anything will come of it. But mainly, I have a little one of my own to teach.'

Eunice looked down at Christopher, and Terry nodded, so full of pride she could barely stand it.

There was a pause. Suddenly the well of things to say ran dry. 'Well Eunice,' Terry said brightly. 'You must come to dinner one night before you leave town.'

'Have your heard from Julie?' Eunice asked at the same time.

There was another pause. Terry stiffened slightly. 'Julie? No. We – lost touch some time ago.'

117

'Oh.' Eunice blinked sandy eyelashes. 'Well, I see her occasionally.' She seemed complacent that she had kept in touch with Julie while Terry hadn't. Perhaps it was some small victory, after all these years.

'Is she all right?' Terry asked casually.

'Well,' Eunice said, 'she had kind of a rough time after she dropped out of college. Of course, there was her mother's breakdown and all. I'm surprised you didn't know,' she added with a lean smile. 'You two seemed to be such great friends.'

I hate you, Eunice, Terry thought. I've always hated you. 'Well, I didn't know,' she said coolly. 'What kind of rough time?'

'Well!' Eunice gave a little laugh. 'Where do I start? She left college halfway through, to marry some bum. A black mechanic, I gather,' she added delicately. 'He turned out to be a real psycho – even tried to kill her. Apparently she got into drugs. Drifted. For a while she was living in New York. Hazel Riordon – you remember Hazel from Home Ec? – saw her on the street one day, and said Julie couldn't have weighed more than seventy pounds. She was trying to be an actress or something.'

Terry closed her eyes for a fraction of a moment. Julie on drugs. Julie married to a black mechanic. Julie weighing seventy pounds. Julie.

'But I guess that didn't work out either,' Eunice went on to distribute her parcels of information, 'because she's back in California again, living in her parents' old house in Palm Springs.' She paused and smiled. 'Kind of sad, isn't it?'

They were coming home from another business party. It was nine in the evening, but the sky was still light. On the front lawns of the houses they passed, parents were in deck chairs, and shrieking children were trying to outwit the cold spray from garden hoses.

Terry felt foolish and jaded, over-dressed in her short silk cocktail dress and tight party shoes. The evening had been, if anything, worse than usual.

'I'll be so glad to get home,' she sighed, rescuing one of Christopher's baseball cards from between the front seats.

'Yes. You made that clear from the time we walked in, didn't you?' Michael said icily.

Terry looked away.

'Jesus,' he scowled. 'I wish you could make a little more effort. Three times Marina Walsh came up to me and said, Was there something wrong? Why did you look so sad? I finally just said you were like that.'

'Well, you can tell Marina Walsh – ' Terry began furiously, but she had nowhere to go with it.

'Look, I know you don't like Clare and Bill,' Michael over-rode her, 'but they are clients, goddammit, and when they're nice enough to invite us for dinner, why can't you just act like a normal person for once? Smile. Be friendly.'

Terry felt stripped of all protection. She wanted to howl, cry, hit Michael, apologize, beg him to keep on loving her –

'Oh, don't cry,' he said, looking over at her disgustedly. Then, more patiently, he began again. 'All I'm saying is why can't you make an effort? You're stuck alone with nothing on your mind but Christopher and that damned play group – and it's making you, well, a little narrow.' He looked sidelong at her. 'And I know you could be the sharpest and smartest woman at any party, if you wanted to be. Look, honey, Marina was talking tonight about this political discussion group she's started – why don't you join? Do you good. You'd make some friends.'

'I don't want any friends!' she longed to cry. 'I just want it to be you and me and Christopher!' But she leaned her head on the sunset-warmed window and said nothing.

'As a matter of fact, I had news of a friend today,' she told him at last, her voice muffled. 'About Julie. She's not doing well. I want to invite her to stay with us.'

Michael frowned. 'Julie? Julie Adams? But you haven't seen her in years.'

Terry shut her eyes. There was a pain behind them. 'Well, I want to see her now.' Michael was silent. 'You just said you want me to have friends, Michael.' Her voice rose. 'Julie's my friend. My only friend. I want to see Julie.'

CHAPTER FOUR

Julie left the Plaza Hotel and began walking mindlessly down Fifth Avenue. But the words Theresa had spoken, as she had thrown Julie from her room, kept vibrating in the air.

Get out. Get out. Get out.

Finally Julie was so exhausted she knew she must sit down. She found a bar on West 48th Street. The music was playing very loudly, making the floor shake. When Julie came in, the bartender glanced up, a little mystified by her. But she sat down casually at a table and ordered a Campari soda.

When her drink came, Julie sipped it slowly. She would not have another, knowing that a second helping of anything diminishes the pleasure of the first. She shivered from the warm touch of the room on her chilled skin. She did not want to leave. From the outside, the bar had looked comforting with the heat of a hundred anonymous bodies, and Julie was cold in her light cashmere coat. At the back of her mind, she wondered if this was a symptom – this being so cold all the time – but she told herself to stop it. Quickly she drank more of her Campari.

Soon there was a man edging from the back room and standing by her table. He was middle-aged, with a bland eggshell face, and wearing a pathetic polyester sports coat. His dyed black hair was arranged in strips over his scalp, and from a distance it looked like the grill marks on a very pale hamburger.

'Can I buy you a drink?' His voice was high, almost grotesque.

Julie was about to refuse, and then an alien voice in her

head said, 'But you know this is your last chance.' She shuddered with surprise. What did that mean? What was she thinking of? She was insane.

She was not aware that tears had come into her eyes, but the man saw them and was touched. He had a daughter like Julie, a sweet girl who also cried at every little thing. 'Let me buy you a drink,' he said again.

'All right,' she said. The thought of being alone appalled her.

The man sat down beside her. His polyester trousers rustled. 'Forgive me for saying it,' he told Julie softly, 'but you don't look like the sort of woman who belongs in this sort of place.'

'I'm the sort of woman who doesn't belong anywhere,' Julie said with an odd, brittle smile.

'Oh, come on now,' he shook his head, 'I bet you have a husband at home. Am I right? And you two had a lover's quarrel. And he's probably going crazy looking for you.'

'No,' Julie said. 'My husband stopped looking for me a long time ago.'

The man frowned. 'Then he's a bum.'

Julie smiled. 'Actually, he's a count.'

The man's voice rose higher. 'No kidding? A count? Where from?'

'Rome.'

He looked at her, awed. 'You're not going to believe this,' he confided, 'but of all the places in the world to go to, Rome is the one my wife has always been dying to see. Isn't that something?' Then he grew flustered, for he had certainly not meant to mention that he had a wife.

A little spasm passed over Julie's face. She put her hand, small and perfumed, on top of his. 'Then you must take her to Rome,' she told him gently.

The man looked away, embarrassed, from their two incongruous hands on the tabletop.

Julie took the last sip of her Campari. She felt very tired

suddenly, very sad, very empty. 'It's so late,' she said. 'I'm afraid I must be going.'

'Oh, no,' the man told her with sad dignity. 'You really don't have to do that.' And he bowed to her and went away himself, fading once again into the fusty obscurity of the back room.

For a moment Julie was sorry he had gone. The grey shape of fear sprang on top of her back again, and no matter how she twisted, she could not see it face to face and fight it. Then the door opened and a tall short-haired woman came into the bar. Julie's first thought was that it was Theresa, coming to find her. It was not. Why should it have been? Yet Julie was sickened at the disappointment she felt.

A moment later, there came along another man. This one was young and sharp. His name was Greg. He sat beside Julie with his long broad legs spread apart. There was not much conversation. Julie broke her rule and had another glass of Campari. As she drank, Greg gently squeezed the back of her throat and watched her swallow. When they were ready to leave the bar, it was raining hard. The pavement was black and treacherous, and glittered from the headlights of passing cars. They took a taxi to Greg's apartment.

Greg's apartment was on West 70th Street. Getting out of the taxi, Julie looked incuriously at the blackened, cavernous front door, the shadows alongside it, the skyline of overflowing garbage bins. She was neither afraid nor repelled. She had seen too many places like this before.

She followed Greg in silence along the black hole of the hallway to an antique elevator. When she stepped inside it, a gasp escaped her. The smell was horrifying. It was as though some animal had lain squashed and decomposing for months beneath the floorboards.

The elevator reached the third floor and she followed Greg along more damp halls. His apartment was large, old, filthy. The living room was slipcovered in dirty clothes, and empty record jackets littered the floor like the stamp collection of a little boy giant. On the table in the kitchenette was an aluminium pot with a half-eaten portion of canned spaghetti crusted along the sides. A dinner fork stuck upright in the congealed mess.

Julie needed a cigarette badly. She stood by the window and smoked, looking out at the twinkling Park below her. 'A Midsummer Night's Dream' could almost be taking place there now. She smiled coldly. More likely a murder was going on, but even so, the sight of those gay paths and lights felt somehow cleansing to her.

Greg came up beside her and crushed out her half-smoked cigarette. He led her into the bedroom. It smelled of hairspray and a stopped-up toilet. Julie sat down on the unmade bed and pulled off her five-hundred-dollar alligator shoes. There was a tiny stain – possibly even a rip – near the toe of the right one. The depression she felt at this was over-whelming. She made herself stop thinking, made herself focus blindly on the present moment and on Greg.

'How much do you pay to live here?' she asked.

He hesitated. 'Seven hundred a month.'

She could tell he was lying, but she couldn't tell whether it was a lie on the high side or the low side. It was diverting to wonder if Greg was the sort of man who wanted to impress her with the money he spent or the money he saved.

'I was just curious,' she said, 'because when I lived in New York, I had a four-room apartment on West Seventh Street for one hundred and twenty dollars a month.'

Greg was not really interested. 'Well, that must have been some time ago.' He pulled her down on the bed and started to caress her ear lobes with his sticky tongue. It was a caress Julie hated.

'Yes,' she said. 'A long time ago.'

She left Greg sleeping on the bed that their combined sweat was now cooling, closed the door of the apartment and hurried back down the hall. But she hesitated by the fouled elevator, wondering if she dared go down the stairs instead. She was feeling very sick. Very sick and very chilled.

A nearby door opened, and a harassed-looking Puerto Rican woman hurried out with a spray can of Pine Room Freshener in her hand. She held the elevator door open and shot out vigorous gusts of spray. The scent of forest glades settled atop the smell of decaying animal.

'My sister is coming by soon,' the woman explained to Julie, her brown eyes moist. 'She makes a visit from San Juan. I want her to see what a wonderful place I live in.'

Julie stood in front of Greg's apartment building, watching in vain for a cab. The rain had slowed to a heavy, damp mist, but Julie had a horror of huddling in the dirty doorway. She stood under a street lamp, her head up. The mist enchanted her hair out of its barrettes and made it stand about her shoulders in a faded golden nimbus.

A young black couple walked by in a cheerful, self-contained embrace. The girl was laughing at something the boy was saying. Julie watched them pass, a half smile on her face.

There was the familiar unpleasantness in her panty hose. She had been in such a hurry to leave Greg's place, and the apartment was so dirty that she hadn't been able to clean herself properly. Finally a taxi came by. Its bright vacant light seemed to mean everything that was childish, simple, happy. Julie flagged it down with a sudden frantic waving of her arms, even though there was nobody else on the street with the desire or even the money to take it away from her.

'The Plaza Hotel,' Julie told the driver.

At first, it was a relief to rest back against the soft, sprung seat – she was so ominously tired. But then she began to perspire; first her hair was a moist cloud, then perspiration began to skid down her arms and under her knees, and finally her whole back seemed to be fused with the vinyl taxi seat.

If I try to get up, she thought, my whole skin will peel off and be stuck to the seat forever.

The Plaza was in semi-darkness – only the lobby was brightly lit. There were few people around at this late hour, and those who were seemed strange. One oddly-dressed young couple was standing over a potted plant and arguing atop its leaves in affected, inebriated voices. They seemed unreal, caricatures of some forgotten Noël Coward play. Julie fancied she could walk right through them.

Her elevator came and Julie pushed the button for her floor. She was exhausted. It was a great relief to lean her throbbing back against the elevator's upholstered wall, but all too soon the sixteenth floor came and it was time to get her body to move once again.

Julie had never told anyone, not even Terry, her first memory.

She was three years old. She hadn't seen her mother all day. At four o'clock her nurse came in and told Julie she was wanted for tea downstairs, and that she was to wear her new dress with the lace collar. Julie ran downstairs and into the drawing room. It was a chilly day and the fire was lit. Her mother looked perhaps more beautiful than Julie had ever seen her. She wore a dark green satin skirt, and her dark hair seemed like part of the flames. Julie started to run to her, then stopped. Across the room, sitting in the armchair, was a man. She did not know who he was. But her mother beckoned to her with such a glowing smile that Julie ran to her and leapt into her lap with a passion of love.

'And this is my little girl,' Julie's mother told the handsome young man. She kissed the back of Julie's neck again and again. Julie grew so excited, feeling her mother's hands stroking her, that all her insides started to tremble. Then she heard a sudden gasp – and before Julie had even realized what had happened, she found herself being pushed roughly away. 'Go back upstairs,' her mother hissed, trying to hide from the young man the sopping ugly stain that had appeared on the satin skirt. 'You've ruined everything.'

Julie was spanked that afternoon for the first time in her life.

Julie had never told anyone her second memory either. She had awakened one night – she couldn't have been more than three and a half – and found she was hungry. She thought of the Cracker Jacks that her parents kept in the projection room downstairs and noiselessly, without awakening her nurse, she crept down the steps. She saw her father on the floor of the projection room. At first Julie thought he was killing a woman. Then she realized that she didn't know what he was doing. She watched for some time, afraid to pass by the two of them to get her Cracker Jacks. The woman saw her first, and gasped. But when Julie's father saw her, he just rolled over and said, 'Think of it as only a movie, kiddo. Kind of like Pinocchio.'

Julie remembered seeing that the woman had a run in her stocking. A tiny little ladder, erupting up the leg. In later years, whenever she heard of Chaos, she was always to think of that ladder.

Julie walked wearily to her hotel room. She felt so faint and it was so hot. Bits of scenes kept coming into her mind. She thought they must be from a play she had acted in, because she knew so many of the lines.

'What are you going to be when you grow up?' Terry was

127

asking her. They were by Julie's pool. Julie was in a bathing suit, but Terry, so proud to be a girl scout at last, had refused to change out of the uniform.

'Well?' she demanded again.

Julie felt terrified. She had no answer, no answer at all. If Terry only knew, she thought. If she only knew how scared I am. And she's not scared of anything.

'Come on – what would you like to be?' Terry asked for the third time.

'You,' Julie whispered into the beach towel.

She was to have dreams about this night for the rest of her life. Waking up from a nightmare – how old had she been? Eight? Nine?

'Mummy! Mummy!' she had called frantically, but her mother hadn't responded. Julie knew she must get out of bed and find her mother, but she was too terrified even to move. Finally she convinced herself that there were alligators under her bed, which would crawl up and eat her if she didn't get out. In a moment, she was running down the black hallway screaming, 'Mummy!' At last she reached the door and wrenched it open. And this was the part she would remember always. The bed was empty.

Julie found her door and walked in. The room was musty. She thought of Greg and his filthy apartment. The smell in the elevator hit her again – oh, God, it had got into her clothes – and she was sick into the toilet.

'Kingdom, phylum, genus, species,' Terry was intoning.

'Terry, do you ever think about boys?' Julie asked.

'Shut up. Osmosis: diffusion through a semi-permeable membrane. No, why should I? We've got a biology test in twenty minutes.' Then Terry put the book down and stared at Julie. 'Why? you don't think about them, do you? You don't, do you?'

128

Julie was silent.

'Oh, come on,' Terry nagged, in the voice Julie was beginning to hate. 'You've got more brains than that. You know what men are. You don't think about them, do you?'

'No,' Julie said. She never thought about anything else.

Julie stood by her window, looking down at the swimming pool below her. The pool light was on, making the water look soft and thrillingly blue. Julie pretended she was somewhere wonderful – Tahiti, maybe – in a beautiful house, looking out at an ocean just this colour. There would be no moon, just the lovesong murmur of waves and palm trees – and behind her a boy would come up and hold her. His arms would be warm and strong.

Julie shivered beside the window.

'I love you,' he would murmur.

'Hurry,' she whispered into the curtains. 'Hurry.'

Julie was too tired to change out of her clothes. She lay in bed, under the covers, trembling with the effort of living.

'Mummy, I'd like to go to the beach now, if you don't mind.'

'Oh, Julie, don't. I'm all alone here. Wouldn't it be more fun to stay with me? We'll play a nice game of Parcheesi.'

'Terry, wouldn't it be fun – just for a lark – to get all dressed up and go to a disco?'

'Fun? Are you crazy? When we've got "The Philadelphia Story" on television? Just hand me some more popcorn, will you?'

She was standing, looking up at a ruined castle on a cliff. It was very cold, and the wind clawed at her cape, demanding entrance. A man stepped from the shadows, and lifted her swiftly on to a low sleigh. Then he sat beside her and three white horses began to draw them towards the castle, to the maddened tune of the sleighbells. He began to kiss her.

'Hurry!' Julie whispered into her pillow.

'Oh, Mummy, please let me go!' Julie begged. 'It's only for five days, and I've always wanted to see New York.'

Her mother shook her auburn head. 'I have a bad feeling about this trip.'

'But, Mummy!' Julie cried. 'The whole Choral Club will be there, and it'll be chaperoned, and Terry will be my room-mate. There's no way anything could happen to me.'

'Well,' said her mother after a long pause. 'All right.'

Julie threw her arms tightly about her mother's neck. 'Oh, Mummy!' she breathed. 'Thank you! I love you! I love you!'

When Julie followed Terry around the streets of New York, she barely saw the big buildings, or the galleries, or even the shops. She was looking for the boy who was to appear – to appear and set her free. It was the first time in her whole life that she was on her own, and somewhere in this City she knew the adventure was waiting.

The moment Julie saw the two boys in the Palm Court, it all came true. 'Terry,' she whispered, 'those two boys over there – they're staring at us!' And it was as if something in Julie had been switched on; a light illuminating a room that was being used for the very first time.

Julie sat on the window ledge of the Plaza Hotel room, her heart beating so excitedly that it stirred the lace on her nightgown. Her whole body felt like a flame. Those boys – those boys coming over and sitting beside her. It had been the most exciting moment of her life.

But Terry! Julie looked pityingly back at Terry, sitting grimly on the bed, eating pretzels and watching television. I feel so sorry for her, Julie thought. She is still such a child. And, with tenderness, because Terry *was* still such a child,

Julie went over to her and sat on the bed and watched television by her side.

And then the 'phone rang. The two girls looked at each other. Slowly, Julie went over and picked up the receiver. It had to be them, she prayed. It had to be. It was.

'We're coming up,' the boy told her.

'Really?' Julie found she was panting. 'Up here? Now?' She could see Terry shoot from the bed.

'No,' she commanded. 'Absolutely not.'

Julie began to perspire. She felt like a trapped animal. 'Well,' she began uncertainly.

'Well?' the boy repeated.

'No!' Terry came over and started shaking her arm. She kept babbling on, but Julie made herself not listen. It was only when Terry said she would tell Julie's mother all about it that Julie snapped back and told the boys not to come up.

But she knew, as she brushed her hair, that they were coming. They had to come. They had to come and set her free.

At three-fifteen in the morning the hotel elevator door opened and Julie tiptoed out. She looked carefully around to make sure that no one from the school Choral Club was lurking in the corridor, but the hallway was empty. All the businessmen and tourists and lovers at the Plaza were asleep.

I shall never sleep again, Julie thought, euphoric. Not after what happened to me tonight. She took the calloused hand of the Puerto Rican boy still waiting in the elevator for her all-clear, and together they went down the hall to her room. Then they stopped and gave each other one deep final kiss.

'You've made my real life begin,' Julie told him solemnly.

He did not understand what she was talking about, and just kept pressing her for another date. But she did not want to see him ever again. No second evening could ever come up to this.

'We'll see,' Julie only said, and kissed him one last time. She had never felt as alive. She would never feel tired again. And yet, how sore she was. Her whole skin was sore – it was the tenderness of the chrysalis bursting all at once, and exposing the butterfly skin beneath.

'Goodbye,' she whispered, and closed the door behind her. The hotel room was in silent darkness. Julie supposed that Terry had cried herself to sleep.

She glanced over at her friend's limp shape on the bed. Suddenly she knew that Terry was only pretending to be asleep. That made Julie angry. She's spying on me, she thought. That's all she's ever done. Spied on everything I've ever thought or felt.

But Terry looked so small and woebegone under the bedclothes that for a second Julie pitied her. For a second she almost told Terry about what had gone on tonight, the greatest night of her life. But she didn't. For Terry, fussy, bumbling, innocent Terry would never understand. To Terry, Julie would always be the little girl in the ruffled pinafore, the first day of the first grade.

But as long as Terry was spying, she would see what she deserved to see. Deliberately, Julie walked into the bathroom, flipped the light on and took off her blouse. She smiled at the strawberry patch of love-bites covering her white breasts. My badges of independence, she thought with a slow proud flush. From Terry, from Mummy, from being 'Little Julie'.

From the bedroom came Terry's gasp as she caught sight of the love-bites and Julie choked back a laugh. Then she began thinking about the two boys who had given them to her until her whole body was one tremor of excitement. She must do something to relieve it. Half-hidden in her make-up case was her diary. Kneeling on the floor, Julie began to write.

There came a stir from the bedroom.

'Julie?' Terry whispered.

The writing stopped.

'Go back to sleep, Terry.'

'What did you do tonight, Julie?'

There was a long pause. Then Julie said evenly, 'Go back to sleep, I said.'

Julie closed the bathroom door so that she could not hear the sobbing.

'Julie, this is it. Our friendship is over.'

It was obviously a rehearsed speech. Terry was trembling all over as she recited it.

'To go off and leave me like that . . . To do what you did with those boys. Only a very immoral person would have done that. I am shocked. Shocked through and through. I obviously don't know you anymore. Maybe I never have.'

'Maybe you never have,' Julie said quietly.

She met him in September of her senior year of high school. His sister Jamie went to ballet class with her, and he came to pick her up one day. Julie could feel him watching her from the moment he came in the door, and he stayed for the entire length of the class. She smiled a tiny smile of triumph at this, because he was not the sort of boy who looked as if he cared much for ballet.

When class was over, Julie got up casually. Slowly, caressingly, she undid the silk ribbons of her toe shoes, slung the bag over her shoulder and walked out. He turned and followed her. His sister had to look elsewhere for a lift that day.

'Marry me, marry me,' he kept murmuring. 'Oh, Julie, you're a goddess. God, you're beautiful. I want you so much. I'll make you happy. Just say that some day you'll marry me.'

Julie played with his blond hair, her eyes dreamy.

Julie was sitting on the gatepost that marked the end of school property. Her hands trembled on the warm stone. She was very happy.

She unbuttoned the blouse of her school uniform until the lace of her brassiere showed. She took off her kneesocks, stowed them in her leather handbag, and put her small feet back into the damp loafers. She freed her hair from its barrette. She did not feel like a schoolgirl now.

From behind her in the auditorium, she could hear the Choral Club practising in pure, cold tones. The sound made Julie uncomfortable. She wondered what punishment she would be given if she were caught cutting classes. But she had been doing it for a month now, and no one had seen her. As if on cue, there was a rustling behind Julie. She turned with a jerk, and there was Terry, ineffectually trying to hide herself behind the gym bleachers. Poor old Terry, Julie thought with exasperation. She's pathetic. She looked away, pretending she hadn't seen.

Julie kept staring at the street, very aware of the anxious myopic eyes still on her. Oh, Terry, she thought. What would you say if you knew what I was doing? For a moment, Julie felt a sharp pang of depression. Terry wouldn't even care. Terry hadn't cared about her ever since that night at the Plaza Hotel. But wasn't that exactly what I wanted? Julie demanded angrily of herself. I outgrew Terry long ago. I have no use for a girlfriend ever again. Yet the depression, almost a sense of regret, persisted. To combat it, Julie made herself think of the boy who was coming to pick her up now. Smiled to think of his smooth, compact body, his curly blond hair. He was a nice boy. Sometimes she almost thought she loved him.

For a moment, Julie let herself be tempted by his offer of marriage. He would be good to her; he would worship her. Maybe it was the right move.

But then she caught herself and laughed. Marry him?

Was she crazy? She wasn't going to marry anybody. End up like her mother? Never. No man was ever going to get the better of her. She would simply use and enjoy them – enjoy them on her terms, for as long as she wanted them.

Her contentment swelled. All around her, it was as if the warm wind, the rustling trees were repeating the words of that magic mirror: 'You are the fairest of them all.'

Oh, God. Life was fantastic. She was free. She was wanted.

And a dented red Volkswagen slid to a stop in front of the gatepost. The door opened and Julie got inside.

'Mummy, what's wrong?' Julie asked anxiously, stroking her mother's head.

'It's you,' Mrs Adams whispered from the bed. 'You seem so faraway.'

'Oh, Mummy, I'm not!'

'We don't talk the way we used to. Remember when we would stay up half the night talking?'

'Sure, Mummy,' Julie said, 'and it'll be that way again. It's just that I have so much homework these days, and school is keeping me so busy.'

'You were late getting home today,' her mother complained. 'I thought we could go to Walter's and have some tea cakes.' She looked up sharply. 'But now it's too late.'

'I had biology lab this afternoon,' Julie said smoothly.

'I see,' Mrs Adams said hesitantly, and then she brightened. 'I'm very proud of my little girl for being such a scholar,' she said finally.

Julie said nothing.

Julie drove her white Oldsmobile rapidly up the driveway to her house. The winter day was cold, but she had opened the windows to numb the headache which had been gathering speed ever since she had left school that afternoon. She felt a strange anxiousness. She did not know why.

She had cut her eighth period study hall that afternoon in order to see Calvin, the boy she had met the day before at Baskin Robbins. They had driven up to Coldwater Canyon, but Calvin's kisses had felt like smog in Julie's throat, so breathless and restless did they make her. The queer, frightened feeling had begun then, and she had asked to be taken back to school. Calvin had fought with her, said she was a tease, but finally he took her back. He drove dangerously, and Julie thrashed from one side of the seat to the other. He didn't even say goodbye when he left her next to her car in the school car park. He gunned the motor and was gone.

But it was no relief to come home. For when Julie pulled up in front of the house, it seemed to her that something there, too, was wrong. It seemed so quiet. She got out of the car and opened the front door noisily. 'I'm home!' she called.

There was silence.

'I'm home!'

Still no answer. Julie frowned. Since the first day of first grade, her mother had been there to meet her at the door when she came home from school. Always.

Julie went anxiously from room to room. They all smelled sweet from furniture polish and all the lights were on, but there was no answer to her calls.

At last she came to her mother's bedroom. The door was open. Mrs Adams was sitting up in her bed with the satin sheets and quilted headboard. And all around her in a circle were ranged Julie's toys – stuffed bunny rabbits, her Sambo doll, Bozo, Pepi, the family of mice, the Koalas. Some of them were toys from babyhood which Julie did not even remember. She stared at them now, with growing fear.

In her mother's white hands with the scarlet nails was Julie's green and white diary. Julie's breath grew quick as she saw it imprisoned there.

'It's too late,' her mother said. 'I've read it.'

With a whimper, Julie started to go to her, but Mrs Adams shrank away as if she were something foul. 'Go away, harlot!' she hissed.

Julie, babbling, tears dripping from her eyes, again tried to go to her; but this time it was the toys which prevented her. On the bed they sat, their cold eyes passing judgement upon her, an unforgiving tribunal that she could not pass.

Julie had to re-dial the number three times, her fingers were jerking so. And when the connection was finally made, each unanswered ring seemed purposefully malevolent, like someone spitting in her face. Finally, on the eighth ring, Terry picked up.

'Julie?' she asked incredulously when she realized who it was. They had not spoken on the 'phone for many months – ever since the night at the Plaza.

'It's Mummy,' Julie whispered. Those two words were such an effort that she had to stop. 'She's taken pills.'

Terry's frightened gasp seemed to make the situation even more real, even more horrible. 'Is she all right?'

'I don't know,' Julie whimpered. 'They took her to Cedar Sinai. I came in the ambulance with her, but they won't let me see her. Oh, Terry,' she gasped between gritted teeth. 'Please come.'

Fifteen minutes later, a tall boney shape came stomping along the hospital corridor. In her hurry to get there, Terry had put on her blouse inside out and her unbrushed hair looked like a clump of corn husks. Never had she looked more wonderful to Julie.

Julie ran to her, sobbing, her bones brittle as a bird's within the nest of Terry's arms. 'Thank God you're here!'

'What are best friends for?' Terry asked gruffly.

Julie burst into fresh tears. 'I don't deserve to be your best friend,' she gulped. 'I know I've been horrible to you these last months – it's just because I've been ashamed. I've done these horrible things – oh, Terry, you don't know.

Things with boys. I knew they were wrong. But I just kept on doing them. And now I'm going to get what I deserve. I know Mummy's going to die, and I'm the one that killed her. We – we had a fight this afternoon.' Her voice, slopping and quivering, did not sound like it belonged to a human being. 'She found my diary. There was stuff in it – all the things I've been doing. She told me to get out of the house – never come back. I drove around a while. But I came back. I thought – I thought – maybe she had changed her mind and would want me again.' Her voice rose to a whispered scream. 'She was in her room. Lying there all dressed up in her satin nightgown. I tried to wake her – she was looking right at me,' Julie covered her face with her hands, 'but she wouldn't wake up.'

'It's all right,' Terry kept saying tensely. 'She's going to be fine. I promise you. Just fine.'

'I've been so bad. I want to go home,' Julie wept, 'and be Mummy's little girl again. I just want it to be the way it was before, with Mummy and with you.'

Terry held Julie more tightly and more tightly until at last Julie relaxed in her arms, and a great silky child-like peace eiderdowned them both. All the months of estrangement shrank away to nothing. And all that was left were Julie and Terry, as they had always been; the team. And behind the panic and the sadness, there was the joy and certainty of that.

'Don't worry,' Terry crooned. 'I'll always be here to take care of you. Always. Always.'

Two weeks later, on an afternoon in early spring, Julie lay on her back on the school lawn. The first bell had just rung for her biology class, but she paid no attention to it.

She was very happy – she felt that the Earthquake had finally passed. Her mother was going to be all right, and everything was safe again. Had she been bewitched? she marvelled, thinking back on the past months of boys and secrecy. Why had she behaved like that? That ridiculous girl wasn't who she was truly. But who was she truly?

And then a memory came to her. She saw herself on an Easter Sunday, running through the Park with a silver filigree basket the Easter Bunny had brought her. And this memory was lit with warm sunshine. That's who I am, Julie thought, smiling. And I must never let anything distract me away from that again.

A large grey cloud passed overhead, making Julie feel quite suddenly grave under its gravity. Yes, there were still problems to be overcome. Her mother, for one. The first thing Mrs Adams had said when she finally came to in the hospital was that she would never, never forgive Julie for the things she had written in the diary. And two weeks later, she was still not speaking to her. 'Give it time,' the therapist kept advising – (the doctors had forced Mrs Adams to go to a psychiatrist three times a week) – 'just give it time.'

But then as the grey cloud gave place to a stretch of blue sky again, Julie's spirits corresponded. Yes, she would give it time, and everything would be wonderful again. Just the way it used to be. And even if her mother failed her, there was always, always Terry. That bossy funny rock, supporting her forever. Tremulously, Julie smiled. I love you, Terry, she thought. I love you better than anyone in the world.

The warning bell rang, and Julie started to rise. Then a footstep on the flagstone made her look up. It was Terry. Julie smiled and impulsively opened her mouth to repeat what she had been saying to herself the moment before. But Terry never gave her the chance.

'Julie, I have something to tell you,' she said. Her face was curiously flushed. 'I could have called you on the 'phone last night, but I wanted to let you know in person.'

Julie raised herself on one elbow. She felt suddenly very afraid. 'Tell me what?'

Terry had trouble beginning. 'It all started in October,' she said, looking away, 'but we weren't close then, you and I, so I didn't tell you about it. I didn't tell anybody.'

'Tell anybody what?' Julie repeated mechanically.

'And then when this thing happened with your mother, I didn't want you to feel like I was deserting you. I'm not, of course,' Terry babbled on, 'it's just that . . . I'm getting married.'

Julie just stared at her.

'His name's Michael,' Terry said. 'Michael Spenser.'

It was all Julie could do to keep from bursting into hysterical laughter.

'He's going to be a doctor,' Terry went on, still not looking at her. 'He's starting at Northwestern in September, and we're – we're moving to Chicago.'

A surge of something like seasickness came over Julie. She felt like she was spinning away from port on to an angry ocean.

'You see,' Terry went on. 'I just found out yesterday. I'm going to have a baby.'

Vomit spewed into Julie's mouth. She swallowed and a raw stream of acid burned her throat. 'The hospital,' she whispered. 'When Mummy took the pills. You told me in the hospital you would be there for me always.'

'Well, Julie,' Terry's voice became very patient, as if she were talking to a child. 'Be reasonable. That was before I *knew*. I mean, I have a baby to think about now, and a fiancé, and though I love you dearly, you really can't expect me to –'

Slowly Julie got up. 'Terry,' she said softly, 'Go to hell.'

Julie looked at the remnants of the crystal vase from Tiffany. Why had she done that? she wondered. Shattered Terry's wedding present to pieces?

She went over to pick up the fragments, and a sharp stab of glass went into her foot. The first stain the blood left on

140

the white rug was gleaming and beautiful; but as Julie began to wipe it away it turned muddy and ugly. Of course, she thought.

She was not sure why she was even going to the wedding. She had not spoken to Terry since that day on the school lawn. But when the invitation came, with Terry's little scrawl at the bottom saying, 'I want you to come,' Julie had known she would.

It was a sad little affair. The day was smoggy and the preacher wheezed and the groom was terribly quiet and Terry too cheerful. Julie could hear her all through the reception, laughing, greeting people, shouting to everyone how happy she was.

Julie thought Terry looked very tired. Pregnancy did not become her. She drank champagne and waited for her turn to be effused at by the rampaging bride. But when Terry finally did catch sight of Julie, she went suddenly very quiet.

She only held her in her arms for a moment and murmured, 'I'm so glad you came. I couldn't bear to leave California without saying goodbye to you.'

A sickening pressure built up in Julie's ears, and for a horrible moment she thought she was going to faint in Terry's arms.

Then Michael came into earshot, and Terry propelled him gleefully over. 'This is *Julie*!' she said exuberantly. 'My best friend.'

'Hello, Michael,' Julie said.

'Hello, Julie,' he answered as quietly.

'I wish you every happiness.'

That he did not answer.

Julie walked into the doctor's waiting room. She was surprised by how large it was, and how many of the girls had brought their boyfriends along. Julie had come alone. She was not even sure which boyfriend it would have been appropriate to bring. She was wearing a dress that was a little too tight. She had used to wear it to Choir performances.

It took nearly an hour for her name to be called. The girl beside her – she had also come alone – couldn't take the waiting. She left after only a little while. Julie could hear her sobbing as she ran down the hallway.

The whole thing took only fifteen minutes. When Julie came out of the clinic into the daylight, the air and sun fell sweetly about her. For a second, she felt like a tiny child again.

That September, Julie started college. On the day she was to leave, she sat for a moment on her bed, dressed in her best skirt and blouse, her two leather suitcases packed and ready on the floor beneath her.

She felt herself cut adrift from all feeling, all energy. She just kept staring around the room. Stripped of its posters, pennants and other teenage memorabilia, it was, startlingly, once again the pink and white bower Julie had known as a child. It gave her a haunted feeling. She half-expected to see Buddo in his old stable by the window, and to hear Terry's bossy little knock announcing that she had come to play.

At the thought of Terry, emotion returned. Julie frowned, and her mouth grew grim and pinched. But she was leaving Terry far behind now, she told herself quickly. She was going off to USC; she was going to make something of herself – while Terry, the ambitious one, was stuck in a little apartment in Illinois, all of her great plans unrealized.

So Terry's life stops there, and here's where mine begins.

On the bookshelf beneath the window was the row of gilded photograph albums Julie had been filling since she was five years old. She would not take them with her to college; she did not want to take any part of the past. But now, in this pale and empty room, the books took on an eerie density and importance. The room seemed like only a stage set for the crowded life within them.

Julie pulled the albums from the shelf in a heap around her. She went hurriedly, guiltily, gluttonously through them. Herself at summer camp. At Christmas. At the Park. In the very first volume was a picture of her father holding her when she was born. It made Julie very sad to see the way he was looking at her. Why, he loved me, she thought. Of course he did. Why did Mummy always tell me he didn't? And there was her first grade class picture. Terry standing beside her, as usual, with the sun full in her glasses. And on the next page was Julie's mother in a black sequin dress at a party. She really is beautiful, Julie thought. Even if she weren't my mother, I'd see it.

On an impulse she dropped the photo album on the bed and stood up. She was going to go into her mother's room and tell her, 'Even if you weren't my mother, I'd think you were the most beautiful woman I've ever seen.' Her heart tripping with absurd excitement, she opened her mother's door, ignoring the pink satin 'Do Not Disturb' pillow on the knob.

Her mother was asleep on the bed, her face covered by a pink satin sleep mask.

'Mummy,' Julie said, sitting beside her and shaking her shoulder. 'Mummy, I'm going off to college now.'

But Mrs Adams slept on. Her unconsciousness shut Julie firmly out. Julie looked down at her. She touched her mother's hand. It was a little brownish, a little crepe-like; but it was still so soft and it smelled so good.

She became aware that Flora, the upstairs maid, was standing by the open door.

'Loudon is ready to drive you, miss, whenever you're ready.'

Julie said nothing. She kept giving her mother's hand little butterfly strokes.

Flora moved closer. 'It's going to feel so empty here without you,' she sighed. 'USC is so close by. Couldn't you change your mind and live at home?'

Julie looked at her mother's bedside table. The little pharmacy vial underneath the lamp showed her that this sleep was on purpose. Damn it, Julie thought. She took a pill so she wouldn't have to see me off. I hate you, she thought.

'Tell Loudon I'll be right there,' she said. 'I just have to get my coat.'

Back in her room, Julie shoved the photo albums away at the top of her wardrobe.

Julie lay awake for a long time that night, in the darkness of her dormitory room. She could see the black shapes of the broken window sash, the built-in desks, the warped table. They already felt familiar. Lazily she watched the earnest squares of light in windows across the quad – eager students were getting ahead with their assignments. And contentedly she listened to the noises in the hallway of her own dorm; showers being taken, teeth being brushed, and the nervous laughter of girls who wanted too quickly to become friends.

Julie turned on her side and looked over at Sara, her roommate. Poor, stupid girl. Since Sara had come into the room, right before dinner, she had told Julie everything about herself; about her brother on drugs, how she hated her father's new wife, and about the boy who had tried to go too far. Then she had added wistfully, 'I hope we'll be real, real good friends.'

That'll be the day, Julie thought, and remembered for a moment that she and Terry had always planned to be roommates at the same college. Then she turned over on her face and put her head in the pillow.

This was the new beginning, she reminded herself. I no longer belong to the past.

One night in late September, Julie was eating dinner alone in the huge college dining room. She had been asked by three different boys if they could eat with her, but she had preferred to be by herself tonight.

Then suddenly she heard someone say 'Hi.' And standing over her, smiling down, were Dorris Halsey and Sandra Fisher, the two most popular girls in the sophomore class.

'Mind if we join you?'

'Not at all,' Julie said casually.

They sat down.

'Tell me,' Doris asked Julie in an offhand way, 'have you given any thought to sororities yet?'

Julie's heart began pulsing with excitement, but 'Not really,' she answered just as casually, deliberately not looking at the small gold Phi Delta Tau pins Dorris and Sandra wore on their lapels.

'Well, it's something to think about, isn't it?' Sandra paused. 'What are you planning on doing after dinner, Julie?'

'Nothing really,' Julie told her, pushing away the thought of tomorrow's history test.

Sandra and Dorris exchanged glances. 'We're going to see the movie in Hall. You want to come along?'

Julie shrugged. 'Sure.'

She looked away, so the girls could not see the victory in her eyes. The Phi Delta Tau sorority was the key to a great many things at USC.

The three girls made their way to the auditorium. The evening had turned sticky and breathless. They bought tickets from a very shy boy who kept looking at Julie. Then they took their seats in the hard chairs.

In the few minutes before the movie began, the girls chatted, and Julie continued to sense the good impression she was making. She saw other students looking over at her, enviously, and she exulted. Her escape from the past was complete now, she kept thinking. She had made it into the best crowd at college.

At last the movie came on. When the titles came up, a faintness flooded Julie. The film was an old-fashioned love drama. The audience had a great time with it. At every melodramatic line the leading lady spoke, they howled with laughter, hissed, whooped. At one point, Sandra and Dorris even started throwing popcorn at the screen.

By the end of the second scene, Julie got up. She ran from the hall, jamming her hand into her mouth, ignoring the calls of the two other girls. She ran across the green steaming quad and up the three flights of stairs to her room. She slammed the door, lay on the floor and sobbed. That had been the film her mother was proudest of.

A letter came for her, in a half familiar hand. When she opened it and saw who it was from, she tore it up without reading it, and threw the pieces in the garbage.

Julie didn't usually go to college dances, because she hated the type of boy who showed up. But tonight she was feeling a little blue, so she stepped in at the Mixer to have a drink.

She noticed the bartender as soon as she came in. The first thing she zeroed in on were his hands. They were long and black and moved with the cool grace of a dancer's.

'What would you like?' he asked her.

'A Pimms Cup Number One,' Julie said, with a challenging smile.

'That's an unusual request at a college dance,' he said. 'We don't have the mix. So I can't give it to you.'

She drew one dainty finger against the shining surface of the bar and looked up at him with wide grey eyes. 'What can you give me?' she asked casually.

He came from Watts. His name was Dwaine and they talked until two in the morning. He was filled with more hate than anyone Julie had ever met. He talked about white people, their greed, their bigotry, their evil, and Julie was shaken. He made her feel ashamed – ashamed that she wasn't poor, ashamed that she wasn't black.

Dwaine's stories of injustice and despair were especially

146

ugly against the incongruous background of gay music and bright dresses. Julie remained motionless on the bar stool. Her dress fell in submissive, yielding folds around her.

He was handsome. One of the most handsome men she had ever seen. And as she drank glass after glass of wine, his hatred began to excite her. When he began striking out against rich girls who knew nothing of life, she knew he was really talking about her. And that excited Julie even more.

'Dance,' he said to her suddenly. 'I want to watch you dance.'

Smiling, she got up. She did not choose as partner any of the boys who had wanted to dance with her all evening; she danced alone, in the centre of the room, with closed eyes and smoothly swaying hair. Julie danced more alluringly than she had ever danced before.

When the dance was over, she came back to the bar and sat down again before Dwaine. And smiled.

The things he showed her that night. Oh, God. Julie was in love for the first time in her life. With Dwaine, she did not have to analyze, or decide. All she had to do was follow. And he never once said he loved her.

There was such a kick in being with him – such a kick in walking down the street, holding his hand and seeing the disapproval on people's faces. Julie revelled in it. She kept hoping they would run into her mother. That would be the greatest kick of all.

'I will show you real life, rich girl,' Dwaine told her. He took her to Watts. She met his sister who was a prostitute and his father who ran the numbers. Julie thought of her safe childhood in the big house, her red Oldsmobile, her pink and white room and she shuddered with shame. She wanted to rip that old self, shackled and spoiled, out of her forever. And the new life, the real life, started now.

Within two weeks, Julie had dropped out of college.

Within a month, she and Dwaine were married. There were no engraved wedding invitations.

'Hello, Gran,' Julie said, walking into her grandmother's spacious apartment in Santa Barbara. Bending gently down, she kissed the tiny woman.

Her grandmother returned her embrace with sombre welcome. 'Where is your husband, child?'

'He's in the car, Gran. I told him to wait outside so we could talk first.'

'There's a lot to talk about.'

'Yes, Gran.'

'When you called last night and said you had got married, I was up for hours trying to think of what to give you as a wedding present. I decided you should have that set of Wedgwood you always loved as a child.'

Julie, to her confusion, found she was beginning to cry. Partly because she loved the Wedgwood and the memories it brought, partly because she had been so hoping that the gift would be money.

'Your mother also wanted the Wedgwood,' her grandmother went on, 'but she had everything in those days, and I didn't see why she should have this, too.'

Her voice was light and steady. Only the trembling of the hand that held her cane showed that her daughter meant everything to her. 'Have you told her, Julie?'

'Yes, Gran,' Julie said coolly. 'She says she never wants to see me again.'

The trembling increased so much that her grandmother had to sit down. 'Julie, forgive her. She's not a well woman these days. She doesn't mean it.'

'Whether she does or not,' Julie was pale, 'it doesn't matter to me. It hasn't for some time now. She's part of my old life.'

'And there's no room for her in the new life?'

Julie shook her head. Her grandmother sighed. She made an effort to speak lightly, charmingly. 'Tell me about Dwaine,' she smiled. 'Is he handsome?'

'Yes; very.'

'Does he work at anything interesting?'

'He's a mechanic. He tends bar at night. He wants to own a body shop one day.'

Julie spoke with deliberation, knowing what effect this was having on her grandmother.

'Can he support you?'

Julie lowered her eyes.

'Your mother's disinherited you, hasn't she, child?' her grandmother asked quietly. 'Yes, I thought so.' She sighed. 'I can't give you any money, Julie. I can't because your mother would not wish me to. And my first loyalty has to be to my daughter.'

Julie, head lowered, kept pushing her index finger through the cut work lace of her grandmother's tablecloth. She wondered dully what she should do. Scream insults? Stamp out? But she was too humiliated to do anything.

'Dwaine must be suffocating in that car,' her grandmother said. 'Why don't you call him in?'

Dwaine came in and they had tea with dainty cakes and cucumber sandwiches. It was a short visit. No one talked much, and Dwaine said nothing at all. At the end of the stay, when Dwaine carried the set of Wedgwood out to his bruised brown Chevy, Julie's grandmother took her arm. Her eyes were dark with unhappiness.

'What have you done, child?' she whispered. 'My God, what have you done?'

Roughly, Julie wrenched her arm free and ran to the car.

Julie and Dwaine walked stiffly into their tiny, stinking apartment on Hollywood Boulevard and Manhattan. They were not speaking. Julie was clutching the large parcel of Wedgwood. Holding it with one hand, she switched on the light. A naked bulb lit up the room – the three-legged sofa propped up by a block of wood, beer crates serving as tables, the lid from Taster's Choice instant coffee spilling out the reeking cigarette butts. The ideal newly weds' cottage.

Dwaine went into the bathroom. Julie knew what he did in there, though they didn't talk about it. When he came out again, his eyes were opaque. He went to the kitchen cabinet and took out a bottle of vodka. He poured some into one of the unwashed juice glasses left in the sink. Even in the act of pouring vodka, he was graceful.

And Julie hated him for it now. As she hated him for everything.

She whirled away from him, ran into the bathroom and slammed the door. She searched for what he had been using, until she found it behind a loose tile. 'All right, you bastard,' she whispered. 'Let's see what it does for me.'

Several minutes later, Julie was sitting on the edge of the bathtub, her head between her hands. Nothing, she said to herself. No peace, no peace. Nothing but hate. Nothing but hate for that filthy bastard.

She lurched back into the living room. 'You lousy bastard,' she said. 'You behaved like a lousy bastard with my grandmother. They're going to lock you up some day.'

She turned from Dwaine and started to unpack the contents of the cardboard box. He was over in two strides, grabbing her by the arm. His fingers were like icy handcuffs on her small wrists.

'Don't touch that,' he said. 'It's going back where it came from. I don't need any of your grandmother's fucking charity.'

'Is that so?' Julie demanded. Jerking her arm from his, she continued to pull back the lid on the box, lifted out a salad plate and dusted it gently. 'It seems to me we could use all the charity we can get.'

But she quieted down the moment she turned and looked into Dwaine's eyes. She got scared. Very scared. They were mad eyes. 'Gran only gave us the dishes because she wants us to be happy,' she whispered.

'You liar!' he cried, and grabbed her tightly by the shoulders. 'She gave us the dishes because she thinks that I'm a fucking nothing.'

Julie recoiled from him, the salad plate still in her hand.

'Put that thing back in the box,' he said slowly. 'You're sending it back to the old hag right now.'

A wildfire anger began to surge through Julie. 'No,' she said, 'I won't. You *are* a fucking nothing, you know that? A fucking nothing!'

Dwaine grabbed the plate out of Julie's hand and smashed it against the wall. The pieces flew about like elegant, deadly icicles. In his hand, like a dagger, was one long sliver. He looked down at it. Musingly, he took Julie's arm again, pulled her to him and held the sliver against her throat. He drew it gently across the veins in her neck as if he were tickling her with a feather. Little beads appeared in a ruby necklace.

'Now, little girl, what are you going to do with the dishes?' he asked gently.

Julie tried not to scream. She tried to stop her shoulders from shaking for fear the stiletto would slide inside her. 'Send them back to Gran,' she whispered.

With a benevolent smile, he released her. Julie shot through the front door, shrieking. She ran down the hall for help, glassy-eyed, incoherent. By the time the neighbours came and broke down the door, they found Dwaine in the middle of the floor, chuckling, surrounded by a three-foot pile of shattered Wedgwood.

The divorce was arranged very quickly. Julie never saw Dwaine again.

In May, Julie moved to a tiny apartment in Santa Monica with glitter on the ceilings and dark green rugs. She hated it, and spent as little time as possible there. She hated the way she felt when she was in those two rooms – as if she had been somehow devalued as a person. There was very little furniture – she had no interest in fixing the place up – but one day in a thrift shop, Julie found posters of two of her mother's movies, and these she hung by her bed. She looked at them often.

Julie had never before realized what a problem not having money was. It amazed her to find out how much it cost to do simple things – like have a dress cleaned. One day she went into Robinsons and unthinkingly asked for a bottle of her favourite deodorant. It took half the money in her purse. The next time she stood in line at Thriftys and bought Ban. But it depressed her even to see it in her medicine cabinet, and she finally threw it away, unused.

Finally she went to the family lawyer. He had always liked her, had always thought she was sweet. She made sure she wore her most schoolgirlish dress to the meeting. When she cried, he managed to get her rent money, but that was all he could do.

Julie spent a lot of time reading magazines.

It was only when she went out that she felt like her true self. She took good care of her clothes, and her well-cut trousers and designer silk shirts still got her respectful glances, and this was the oxygen Julie breathed. Some nights she worked for half an hour, getting the lint off her black Ralph Lauren skirt.

One rainy Monday, her Gucci scarf was taken by the wind, and a bus ran over it.

'Oh, just leave it,' Julie said airily to a young girl who was prepared to run across the street and rescue the torn rag. 'It's only a scarf.'

She told herself that night that she was stupid to cry.

On Julie's eighteenth birthday, Terry went into Marshall Fields and picked out a tiny bottle of Antelope, Julie's favourite perfume. Julie used the whole bottle up in one day.

★

Julie tried only once to get a job. One day she went into Frank Safford's antique shop on Melrose. It was a place she and her mother had always loved to browse.

'Why, little Julie,' Mr Safford beamed, coming from behind a cave of Louis Fifteen sofas and chairs. He was a tiny, fragile man. 'I haven't seen you in so long. How is your dear mother?'

'She's all right,' Julie said carefully. 'Listen, Mr Safford – I have a favour to ask.' She blushed painfully. She did not like asking favours. 'Things have changed. I need a job. Would you give me one?'

She had thought he would say yes right away – he had always seemed so fond of her – but he only stared at her with worried puzzlement. 'But do you know anything about antiques?' he asked her, with a strange, rather ugly smile.

Julie was silent.

'I mean, it's one thing to buy them. It's quite another to work in a shop that sells them.' And he gave a dry little laugh.

At that moment, Anne Scully came into Mr Safford's store. 'Julie,' she said. 'My God. I haven't seen you since Graduation!'

'No,' said Julie cooly, hoping that Anne didn't recognize her cashmere suit from those days.

'What on earth have you been doing?'

'A great many things,' Julie said.

'May I help you, miss?' Mr Safford had come forward, once again the genial, unctuous proprietor Julie had always known.

Anne was all business. 'Yes. I'm looking for a Tiffany lamp. My fiancé absolutely has his heart set on them, so I'm trying to find one as a wedding present.'

While Mr Safford went into the back room to search his stock, Anne turned to Julie. 'You look wonderful,' she said, and simpered. 'It just goes to show.'

'Goes to show what?' Julie asked coldly.

'Oh, just that you can never listen to gossip.'

'About me?'

'Oh, well. Some of the girls were saying that you were in a pretty bad way.'

'As you pointed out,' Julie told her, 'you can never listen to gossip.'

Anne glanced around the shop. 'This is such a darling place. What are you looking for?'

Mr Safford returned then, bearing his Tiffany lamp.

'Why, that's perfect,' Anne began, but Julie rode over her.

'Oh, I'm so sorry, Anne,' she said sweetly, 'but I'm afraid Mr Safford has made a mistake. I asked him to put this lamp on hold for me – and I'm buying it.'

It was over very quickly. Under Mr Safford's astonished eyes, Julie dashed off a cheque for an amount that emptied her bank balance. Then she nodded coolly to Anne and left the store, the Tiffany lamp under her arm.

One evening Julie found herself near USC and impulsively she pulled in. There was still a college sticker on the car, so she parked in the student car park. She felt queer being there again, wistful. She wandered around the halls. Even though she had only been gone a short time, the students looked a lot younger than she remembered. Finding there was a showing of 'Casablanca' that night, Julie went through her wallet. Yes, she still had her student ID and movie discount ticket. She walked into the classroom used for the screening, and sat down at one of the desks. It felt wonderfully carefree being a student again – as if all the rest had been a dream.

In a few minutes though, someone recognized her and pointed her out to the proctor, and Julie was politely asked to leave.

For the first few months after her divorce, she was totally

alone. She had a 'phone put in the apartment, and automatically opted for the model with the most expensive gimmicks. But the 'phone never rang. It was an eerie feeling, not speaking to another human being, sometimes for two days on end. She read more magazines, took walks along the Venice beach. She thought about suicide a lot.

A lot of men approached her, but Julie was not interested. After Dwaine, she told herself, she had had enough.

But then, one cold night in June, she stopped into an Irish bar on Santa Monica Boulevard. The place was full of people Julie's age; they were laughing and slightly dirty. Their eyes were dim with drugs. They looked like they were having a good time. When one of the boys asked Julie to join them, she shrugged. 'Okay,' she said, with a slight smile. She should have known that she was not the sort to stay lonely for too long.

What Julie remembered mainly from those months that followed were the bars, the emptiness, and the intense relationships that lasted only a few days. And the parties. There were always parties, it seemed, taking place any time; strange amoeba groupings that dispersed and re-gathered in different locales. Sometimes there were changes in the group. Often one of the regulars died of a drug overdose, and that was certainly very sad. But there were always others to fill the void.

One night in October, she visited a new place. The Miltons' apartment had once been part of a warehouse downtown, and it still smelled faintly of stamp gum and printer's ink. The ceilings were painted black and the furniture, streamlined, fibreglass, and coloured either a vivid yellow or red, gave the impression that the room was filled with oversized Lego pieces.

It was Julie's first time there. Alison, one of the girls she knew, had brought her. Alison said that this was the most exciting crowd in town.

Julie finished telling the story of Dwaine and her grandmother's Wedgwood dishes to the most exciting crowd in town. 'And when we finally got the door open, there he was – up to his knees in broken china.'

She looked around, wanting signs of horror or amusement or interest, but there was nothing. Lined against the wall, three young girls were shooting up. A young blond painter began making love to Alison. Two bald men in leather slacks had switched on the stereo and were dancing a tango, mouth to mouth.

No one had even been listening to Julie's story. No one had heard. Tears filled Julie's eyes. Tears of self-pity, self-hate.

What was she doing here? she wondered. What the hell was she doing here? She looked at the scene around her and felt as dirty as she had ever felt in her life.

The tears were tasting more and more corrupt. Julie thought of her grandmother. She thought of the Wedgwood, and how rare and beautiful it had been before it was broken. And she started to keen in a high, weak wail.

'Mummy?'

Mrs Adams was in the drawing room of her enormous house. She sat very straight. All the furniture was swathed in dropcloths, except for the sofa she was sitting on. It was of creamy blue satin and it looked like a piece of doll's house furniture.

'Mummy?' Julie said again.

She was dressed in her best white suit, and there was no make-up on her face.

'Sit down,' her mother said in her most gracious voice. She motioned towards one of the swathed chairs and upon this Julie sat.

'What's the weather like?' Mrs Adams continued brightly.

156

'I thought I might visit the Van Gogh exhibit at the Art Museum if it's fine out.'

'Mummy,' Julie said tremulously. 'I've got to talk to you. Thank you so much for seeing me. I know I'm horrible. You were right in everything you said. But I'm paying for it now. There's nothing good in my whole life. Please, Mummy –'

Mrs Adams nodded thoughtfully. 'But if it's hot, there's nothing more distressing than walking along those museum grounds. You begin to fancy that those plaster dinosaurs in the tar pits are real.'

'Mummy,' Julie said in a louder voice, 'please give me another chance. I want to come back home. I want things to be like they were before.'

Her mother took a delicate sip from her teacup. 'I've always felt especially sorry for the mammoth out drowning in the tar. I've always imagined that that was the mother, and the other was her baby left back on shore. Sad, isn't it?'

Julie went over and buried her hot face in her mother's cool lap. 'I'm sorry, Mummy!' she cried. 'I'm sorry! I'm sorry!'

'On the other hand,' her mother said, thoughtfully dropping a lump of sugar into the teacup, 'if it's a rainy day, I often enjoy going to the Planetarium.'

Julie moved to New York that fall. She decided she was going to be an actress. She found an apartment in the West Village, negligible with regard to both size and charm, and shared it with Marguerite, a woman she had met at her acting class. The two of them got along well. They were rarely home.

Paying the rent proved to be not too much of a problem. Julie made men friends very quickly in New York, and she preferred rich ones.

One night Marguerite came home and asked if Julie would like to come with her to a cocktail party the following

Friday. She said a lot of people useful to their careers would be there. Julie accepted. Marguerite, when she saw how stunning Julie looked in her new Ralph Lauren dress, seemed regretful that she had invited her.

The party was held at Automation House on Park Avenue. It was terribly noisy in the small rooms and off-puttingly crowded, but Julie liked the feeling of being helpless in the wave of people. She was finally cast ashore in the far corner of the downstairs room where a man was standing.

He was in his fifties, small, compact, and fiercely tanned. His hair was clipped short like a Roman's and there was something of the look of a Caesar in his sated, slightly-bulging grey eyes. He wore the most expensive suit in the room.

'I've been watching you,' he said. His voice was as polished as steel. 'You've got something, you know. Yes. I see you do know it.'

'I'm happy to meet you, too,' she said.

'I'm in a position to do you some favours,' he said.

'I know,' she said.

He put a cold hand matter-of-factly to her neck and squeezed it. Julie closed her eyes. 'I have a car outside,' he told her. He did not remove his hand. 'Are you coming?'

'Aren't you even going to ask me my name?' she said. 'It would be civilized to do that, don't you think?'

He smiled. 'What is your name?'

'Julie Adams.'

'Adams is my name, too,' he told her.

'That's because you're my father, you bastard,' she said, and was gone.

Marguerite said she would call the hospital if Julie didn't stop crying. Julie finally stopped.

It was 1.45 on a sulky hot afternoon in August. Julie had a

2.00 audition for an off-Broadway show. She stood at 73rd and fifth, willing, with gritted teeth, an empty taxi to come by. None came.

The audition was on 48th Street. Julie cursed herself for being so disorganized. She began to walk, then to run. The hair which she had just had blow-waved dry began to sag. Her silk blouse clung in damp patches to her back. She was not aware of the limousine until it had swum like a great black shark directly beside her. It stopped, and the back door opened. A single man was inside. He was not young. His hair was silver, and beneath it, his face was as tensely full of angles as a canvas by Bracque. Oddly enough it was the Count's clothes which first attracted Julie to him. It had been a long time since she had seen anyone in a dark grey suit, white shirt and conservative silk tie. It brought her back to the world of her childhood, in which people had dressed for parties. She wondered where this man was going.

'Let me give you a lift,' he said. He spoke with an accent.

Julie noticed that the limousine had black, one-way windows. If I got in and he tried to kill me, she thought, I could scream my head off and no one would ever even know.

And it was this that decided her to get into the car. She never made it to the audition.

They were walking through Central Park late at night. With him, she was unafraid.

'Marry me,' the Count said again. His dark eyes looked irridescent like an oil slick on the road.

'No.' Julie flung her hair petulantly back. 'It would be crazy. You're a Catholic, I'm not, there'd be my divorce to explain to your family, and you expect me to go off and live in Italy. Maybe I just don't want to let myself in for all that.'

She pushed his hand away from hers, her mouth trembling slightly. She was mad about him; yes, yes, she adored him. Since they had met, he had swept her life clean of anything but himself. His voice on the 'phone, the smell of him, the huskiness of his touch. But never would she let him know.

'These are things that can be dealt with.' The Count pulled her against him easily with dark heavy hands. Even after three generations of family riches, the rough vineyard-growing strains had not been effaced from the shape of those fingers.

And he went on to tell her about the villa she would be mistress of, the clothes he would buy her on their honeymoon, the parties they would give together. And he told her how everyone would worship her.

Julie stood, tiny and arrogant, before him. 'Why do you love me so much?' she asked finally.

He looked at her narrowly, at her hair rough as a playing child's, at the loose careless dress she wore, and thought of the untidy Village apartment where she lived. 'I will be your haven,' he said.

And her small head lolled forward against his chest. She had not had a haven since Mummy and Terry. She began to cry.

The Roman sun fell, cynical and wan. Julie was alone in the Castello, waiting for the Count to return from his weekly card game. She wandered restlessly from room to room of the enormous, ornate palace he had brought her to. In every chamber there was at least one servant, dusting, straightening a rug, turning down a bed. They greeted her in Italian with hushed respect. Julie liked that.

She was very happy in her new life. There was a limousine to take her to the boutiques on Via Borgognone, Via Frattina and Via Contotti whenever she felt like it. She felt like it nearly every afternoon. Already the saleswomen in the stores were beginning to treat with deference the tiny blonde American who said so little and bought so often.

And afterwards Julie would spread all her new clothes on the bed and gloat over them. They pronounced, with every flawless seam, with every hand-sewn stitch, that once again she was special – that once again, she was herself.

Julie was less happy with the rest of Rome. The wildness of it terrified her; the suave cruelty in the faces of the men, the poverty, the naked emotionalism. And there was something almost unbearable about the Catholic churches everywhere, with their sere-faced plaster saints and opulently hung walls. Yet every time Julie passed one, she was always compelled to go into it. She did not know why.

But when she was with the Count, she did not go into any churches. They went to parties, extravagant, fanciful parties where the food was delicious and there was always music to take the place of thought.

There was always some young man at these parties, perhaps a film star or wine magnate, who would become inflamed by Julie. There would be a series of impassioned calls in faulty English, child-like letters, pleas for a meeting. But Julie, for the first time, had found a man she did not want to cheat on.

The sunset was growing richer now, adding a palette of almost unbearably beautiful oranges and rusts to the southern landscape. Julie watched it from the window; then she sighed and turned back to the darkening room. She wished her husband would come home. She felt as lonely and vulnerable as a child. She tried to read a paperback she had bought that day at the American bookshop, but the creeping unease continued. Finally she thought of the television. It was an antiquated black and white set she had unearthed from one of the downstairs closets. She had not watched it in the month she had been here, because she spoke no Italian. But tonight, in the closing dark, she needed to hear another voice.

She flicked the dial nervously, and on the very last station, the titles of 'I Love Lucy' shot on to the screen.

Julie gave a little gasp of joy. The voices dubbed in Italian did not matter. It was Lucy! And Julie was fifteen again, lying on the bed of the Plaza Hotel room with Terry, eating popcorn and waiting for life to happen.

The shadows in the room swelled. Julie laughed wildly at the show again and again. Again and again in the huge, elegant parlour.

The front door slammed. 'Julie, I'm home!'

Julie stood up. She paused a moment before the set, wanting to show the Count the treasure she had recovered from childhood. Then she bent and snapped the television off. For what possible relevance could 'I Love Lucy', and all that she meant to Julie, have for the Count? None. Of course none. And for a moment Julie wondered what in Heaven's name she was doing here, so far away from home.

'Julie!' he called again.

Julie shivered. Her husband's voice sounded like that of a stranger.

They were coming home late at night from a party. The Count had bought a red Masarati the week before, and this was the first time he had driven it. He drove aggressively, but well. It was the way he did most things. Suddenly there was a shrill, confused smash of lights and sound. The Masarati squealed indignantly to a stop. A young man on a motorcycle without lights had sideswiped the car, and there was a tiny dent along one of the fenders.

Slowly the Count got out of the car. And then, under Julie's disbelieving eyes, he went mad. He grabbed the young man by the throat, and let forth a gutter stream of Italian as he shook him back and forth. Horrified, Julie watched the enjoyment in his face as he thrashed the boy; sickened, she watched him whip and beat and bully. And when he got back into the car, leaving the boy bleeding in the road, he pulled immediately over to the side of the highway.

'Let's make love,' he said. 'Right now. Right here.'

So this is who you really were all the time, Julie thought in cold wonder.

Sometimes it takes years to fall out of love. Sometimes it takes only a second.

It did not come as any great surprise to Julie to find that the Count was cheating on her. In a way she had been expecting it – Julie had never forgotten what her mother had told her about men, that hot night in Palm Springs. But her pride was inflamed to a frenzy. No man had ever cheated on her before, and for a while it almost made her want him again. But the day came when he sought her out, crying and confessing and declaring that he had done what he had only to make her jealous. And Julie's desire withered, as quickly as it had sprung up, and all that was left was weariness.

She told the Count that she forgave him, then broke into his frenzied thanks.

'But there's something I want in return,' she told him.

'Anything, my darling,' he said.

'I want to go back to California for a while.'

He was startled. 'California? But why? You have no family there. No one to see.'

'I have a mother.'

'A mother? You told me your mother was dead!'

'You may go in and see her now,' the smiling nurse said.

Julie followed the nurse through the low, brightly painted corridors of the Motion Picture Home. In a room to the right, a hot gin rummy game was going on between a stuntman who had lost his leg doing a fall for Gary Cooper, and a senile gossip columnist who liked to remember the caption she had put under Fatty Arbuckle's picture when he was hauled in.

163

'Finish up your game, dears,' the nurse told them. 'You don't want to miss lunch.'

'Oh, no!' they chirped.

In the dining room beyond, crowds of old people sat talking at small tables. There were cameramen and stars there, screenwriters and producers' wives. The dining room was like a studio commissary, but in grotesque parody. The cameramen were so arthritic they could not hold their forks, the stars, with perfectly blued hair, had faces wrinkled as sand, the screenwriters were blind and the producers' wives talked about their husbands' films of sixty years ago and could not remember the titles. Julie walked quickly by.

'We've given her lunch on a tray today,' the nurse said. 'So that you can have your visit in private.'

Julie resented the nurse's concentrated stare at her silk jersey dress and the emerald ring the Count had given her for her birthday.

They went down the corridor. Each room was a bright little bead, filled with flowers and cards and pictures of grandchildren on the bedside tables. It all reminded Julie of a college dormitory – at least, some set designer's idea of a college dormitory – where everything was upbeat and secure. There was only one small menace that slipped into this place. Even now, an oxygen tent was being smuggled unobtrusively into someone's gay cubicle.

Julie's mother's room was bare. There were no comforts here, no hand-worked afghans, no photographs, no flowers. Obscurely, Julie felt a great relief. Then the guilt came. She would send her mother a sheaf of roses this afternoon.

Mrs Adams was sitting, dignified and beautiful, on the pressed wood chair. Her hair was still like frozen wheat, her skin still glowed like a rubbed pearl. Only the vagueness in her blue eyes gave evidence of the complete breakdown that had brought her here.

'Look who's come to visit, dear,' the nurse said.

Julie's mother looked at Julie.

'Nurse,' she said, holding out her hand, 'this is my baby. My sweet little girl. This is my Julie.'

'Your mother talks about you all the time,' the nurse said brightly. 'About how you used to chase after the Easter Bunny and she would take your picture. And all your birthday parties and the presents you got.'

Julie closed her eyes in pain and bewilderment. And that was all her mother remembered, was it? All those other years had been wiped out. How convenient for her. Julie felt very old, suddenly, sitting in the room with this smiling child.

'Are you happy here?' she asked carefully.

Mrs Adams nodded brightly, and patted Julie's hair.

'Do you have lots of friends?'

Another nod. Mrs Adams was busy straightening Julie's pretty necklace. Her touch felt at once so familiar and so strange.

'Julie.' Mrs Adams thrust the necklace aside. She straightened up. Her eyes were bright with sudden undeniable intelligence. 'I have something to tell you.'

Utter relief sprang within Julie at this sudden change in her mother. She leaned down eagerly to hear. She melted into a child again, and her hair fell forward on her mother's breast. 'What is it, Mummy?'

'Who do you think is an orderly in this ward?' Mrs Adams whispered.

'Who?' Julie asked.

Her mother smiled very wisely. 'Jesus Christ,' she said.

Julie did not return to Rome. The day she was supposed to fly back, she rented a car at Los Angeles airport, and drove down to her parents' old house in Palm Springs to live.

No place is as quiet as the desert at night. The old house had fallen into much decay. The furniture and colours, once such trendy fun, looked sadly out of style now; and the floors and walls were filled with grit. Julie moved about the silent rooms, dressed in one of her mother's satin nightgowns from long ago. She had many of her own, but they all reminded her of the Count and his touches.

Wearing the nightgown, Julie felt that, in some curious way, she had become her mother. Her mother's smell was still in the maribou at the neck. And there she was at the bar, fixing herself a drink in the heavy Baccarat glass, as her mother had always done. When Julie passed in front of a mirror, she was surprised to see that the face reflected in it was still her own.

How many years had it been since she was last here? Was it really fifteen years ago that she and Terry had listened on a summer night to her mother explode in her hatred against men? That night of revelation. Julie found she could recall it with such an odd clarity. She could even see Terry lying on the floor, doing a jigsaw puzzle. Slowly, Julie went over to the closet. There was the jigsaw puzzle. She opened the box and felt old and afraid because all the pieces were mildewed and warped now.

She went silently around the rest of the house, opening all the drawers and closets. In her own room she found a neatly folded prim pile of tennis dresses. She had worn those at the Racquet Club. How long ago since she had been a little girl there, tanned and content, eating a chicken sandwich and drinking ice tea? And she found a school notebook from eighth grade, with notes to Terry in their secret code on every page. She couldn't remember the code anymore, so the words would be forever undeciphered.

She went into her mother's bedroom. In the bedside drawer were cosmetics, baked dark brown and dry with age. And in the wardrobe were her mother's golden mules.

The doorbell rang. Julie frowned, wondering who it could be. No one even knew she was here. She opened the door cautiously. Outside was a young red-haired policeman. Seeing that she was in her robe, he blushed.

'Sorry to disturb you, Mrs Adams,' he said shyly. Julie did not tell him that she was not Mrs Adams. 'But this house has been empty so long – I saw the lights – I thought maybe it was being robbed.'

'No. I just felt like coming back,' Julie said. 'After all these years.'

The policeman started to go, and then he turned back. 'I just want to tell you,' he said, 'that you look exactly the same in real life as you do in your movies.'

On Christmas Eve, Julie went to a Mass at a little church in Rancho Mirage. The chapel was plaintively simple and still. She looked around her, at the trustful light of the candles and the serenity on the faces of the worshippers. She tried to find God somewhere in the roof above. She did not succeed.

She closed her eyes. The music, the incense was lulling. Yes, perhaps God was there, after all. Perhaps. But when Julie opened her eyes again, she saw that the woman next to her was badly dressed. She saw that the man in front of her was asleep with his mouth open, and that the priest was a hammy actor. And that was all she could see. That was all there *was* to see.

Julie stood up, pushed her way out of the pew and ran out of the side door. God help me, she thought. God help me, as she hurried down the steps.

CHAPTER FIVE

Theresa was in her hotel room dressing for the banquet. She tried to keep her mind on the evening ahead, but she kept coming back to that afternoon's telephone call to Christopher. Christopher. And when that was too painful, she found she was slipping back into the past, when times were golden and sweet, and happy moments flew like leaves into her hands.

Christopher had just had his fifth birthday. Terry was in the kitchen of the apartment doing the breakfast dishes and listening to her favourite country music station. A news flash came on. A renowned scientist had predicted that a meteor was due to fall in the Evanston area at two that afternoon. Terry shook her head sceptically and continued to dry the dishes. Then she paused and began to wipe more slowly.

Suddenly she found herself picking up her handbag with still damp hands, pulling on her coat, and rushing from the apartment building. On a good day, it took her three tries before she got the slightly bruised Volkswagen beetle out of the garage. Today it took her eight.

She drove at a speed far past the legal limit. The roads to Christopher's school were meek and sweet with early spring. The school car park, without the paraphernalia of lollipop men and school buses, looked amazingly empty. As though a bomb had fallen. Or a meteor!

Terry found the kindergarten after several minutes of searching. It was milk-break, and the teacher, Mrs D'Amato was alone in the room.

'I've come to take Christopher home,' Terry told her.

'I hope nothing's wrong,' Mrs D'Amato asked with delicate avidity.

'No,' Terry said shortly. 'I just think Christopher would be better off with me today.'

Mrs D'Amato scowled disapprovingly, but she did not have the authority to pursue the subject. 'He's in the playground,' she said coldly. 'Perhaps I had better get him.'

'No, thank you. I'll go myself,' Terry told her, resenting the implication that Christopher wouldn't be willing to come unless his teacher fetched him.

Christopher was by the swing set. Two little girls were tying him to the slide with skipping ropes, and he was squealing with excitement. When he saw his mother, his cries stopped at once. The little girls let the skipping rope drop. Terry felt ridiculous in the playground – her shadow on the asphalt was so much taller than those of the children. She looked like some grotesque Queen of the Fairies.

'Everything all right?' Christopher asked.

'I'll tell you when we're alone,' Terry said impressively, so that he could keep face with the wide-eyed little girls.

But when they got to the car, she felt too embarrassed to tell her son that she had taken him from school for fear a meteor was going to fall on him. 'Nothing's wrong at all,' she said lightly, smoothing the rough gold hair with hands that shook from love. 'I guess I just got so lonely for you I couldn't stand it.'

The two of them spent an enchanted afternoon together, playing bears and Tag and making cookies and building a Lego spaceship. And no falling meteors came to disturb them.

The banquet was being held in the Edwardian Room. Theresa went through the cocktail hour numbly, responding pleasantly enough to colleagues and the women who had been in yesterday's seminar audience. But Christopher was still the tide in her mind. She could no longer summon the happy memories – all she could think of was the conversation on the 'phone this afternoon, and the way he had sounded. Christopher! Christopher! Sometimes the name tolled slowly, mournfully. Sometimes it came with a rushing whir like the dresses of the women as they moved across the room towards her. Sometimes it was like a taste in her mouth, as biting and strong as the vodka and tonic she was drinking. And sometimes it was like the cry of a friend searching for another friend who was lost. Christopher! Christopher!

'Mrs Spenser!' A walking Christmas tree decorated at Tiffany's came across the floor towards Theresa. It was Mrs Eagerman, dressed in green velvet and crammed, ears, nose, and throat, with diamonds.

'I hope you're enjoying our little party,' she cooed. 'I took the liberty of seating myself next to you at dinner. I said, none of this boy/girl nonsense tonight. I'm not going to give her up!'

Absentmindedly, Theresa made the appropriate response.

Finally the dinner was served. The sick numbness grew in Theresa. She had to eat her salad and soup very carefully, because every second or third swallow she took, her throat closed up. Bright little golden lights flickered before her eyes, and she felt herself choking. Tiny bites; tiny sips. That was the way to keep from suffocating. Christopher. Christopher.

Mrs Eagerman talked desultorily to Theresa during the first few courses – what had she done in New York, had she seen any worthwhile plays, had she discovered any marvellous little restaurants? But then when the main course arrived, the chairwoman turned to her with a different light in her eye.

'Mrs Spenser,' she said almost shyly, 'I must tell you. I felt very badly about something that happened between us yesterday.'

170

'Oh?'

'Yes – when I asked you about your husband and you said you had been divorced.'

'Yes?' Theresa said coldly.

'Well, I certainly didn't mean to pry.'

Theresa relaxed. 'Oh. That's quite all right.'

'Is it?' Mrs Eagerman looked up slowly. 'Then could I be so rude as to follow up with another question? I was awake all last night, worrying. I mean, if you could get divorced, what hope is there for all the rest of us girls?' She leaned towards her. Theresa felt awash in the woman's perfume. 'Would you tell me – could you tell me – why you got divorced?' she murmured.

Something inside Theresa snapped. That's really none of your business, she could have said. Or she could have got up from the table and left. But she turned to the chairwoman and said precisely, 'We got divorced because my husband fell in love with someone else.'

That ended the conversation.

At the next day's seminar, the slide projector kept failing, and the meetings were not concluded until four-fifteen in the afternoon. Theresa came out of the conference room at last, blinking wearily, feeling mussed and a little sour in her suit. She was heading towards the bank of elevators to go to her room, when once again she heard the violins in the Palm Court.

Why were they so irresistible?

Slowly, as if in a dream, Theresa came in and let herself be seated at a small marble table. She closed her eyes. She felt a figure appear beside her. Thinking it was the waiter, Theresa lifted her head and looked up. It was Julie.

'I thought you'd come here,' Julie said. 'I've been waiting.'

She was wearing a tight dress, and Theresa could see her ribs like flat, childish Popsicle sticks. She looked away.

Julie sat down beside her. 'The reason I came over,' she said in a cool, even voice, 'is that I've got to go to the doctor tomorrow. And I wanted to know if you'd mind going with me.'

It was lunacy. This absurd, off-hand conversation after all these years. Theresa did not even take in the question for a moment. Then she looked up and was struck, almost physically struck, by the fear in Julie's eyes.

'Is it anything serious?' she asked levelly.

Julie's eyes answered the question.

Theresa shook her head to try and clear it. 'How did you find me?'

'It wasn't hard,' Julie said lightly. 'You're pretty famous, you know.'

'Is that what you're doing in New York?' Theresa asked in sharp bewilderment. 'You came to see me?'

Julie shook her head.

'The doctor?'

Julie nodded. 'Will you come with me?' she asked again.

Theresa looked around the room. Two waiters were having an argument. The old man with the wheelchair and the crème caramel was not there today. She wondered what had happened to him. The flowers in the vases seemed awfully, awfully bright.

The words hovered about her, a miasmic, tight balloon from a cartoon character's mouth.

She did not know why she said, 'All right. I'll come.' And the moment the words were out, Theresa felt pity, such pity – and underneath it all, something else. A black sense of triumph.

That night she remembered Binky Elliot.

Binky Elliot had died of a brain tumour. The sixth graders at Pratt didn't even know she had been sick until one Monday morning the headmistress, looking heavy and helpless, had climbed up to the assembly stage to make an announcement.

'I have some rather sad news . . .'

Terry had never liked Binky Elliot. She thought Binky was very stuck-up just because her father, an important military advisor, got asked to dinner at the White House from time to time. Terry always pretended to be very unimpressed by this. She would even go out of her way to let Binky see how unimpressed she was. Terry thought unhappily of that now.

The funeral was to be held at the church on Wilshire. All the girls in the class were going. The usual Saturday plans and fun were forgotten for this week. Terry sat on the couch in the front room of her house, waiting for Julie to come and pick her up in the limousine. The warm May sun tumbled in the window and puffed out the sleeves on Terry's best white dress. It felt nice and strange being dressed up like this – like she was going to a party. And then she remembered that the reason she was dressed up was because Binky Elliot was dead.

When the limo pulled up and Terry went outside to find Julie also in her finery, it was somehow embarrassing for both of them. They put up the glass partition so that they could have privacy from the driver, but for a long time neither girl said anything at all.

'This makes me think about dying,' Julie said suddenly, at last. 'What about you?'

'Yeah.'

'But Mummy says I don't have anything to worry about,' Julie whispered. 'When she heard about Binky, she looked up all the symptoms of brain tumours in a book, and she said I don't have any of them. Do you want to know what they are?' she added earnestly. 'To make sure you don't have them, too?'

'That's okay,' Terry smiled. 'I know I'm fine.' She looked sidelong at Julie. This was a risky thing to say, because Julie might laugh at her. But she said it anyway. 'You know, Julie, ever since I was a little girl, I've had this feeling – that I'm going to live to be very old. I'm really sure of it. So I don't worry about dying at all.'

Far from laughing, Julie was staring at her with round eyes. 'And what about me?' she demanded. 'What's going to happen to me, Terry?'

Terry blinked. She didn't have a clue as to what would happen to Julie. 'Oh, you'll live even longer than I will,' she said easily.

Julie gripped her with such tension that Terry was taken aback. 'Are you sure?' she whispered.

'Positive,' Terry said staunchly.

Julie sighed with bone-deep relief, and fell back on to the seat.

Once again, Theresa could not sleep, but tonight she did not want to take a pill. At least not yet.

She was looking down at the Park below her. She thought of Christopher – how, as a child, he had loved parks and woods and wild places more than anything. He had been Robin Hood; always little Robin Hood. Wearing the little green cape she had sewn for him, he would shoot his fierce imaginary arrows at her every time she walked by. She made sure she walked by often. She was the Rich, and she had to be made to give to the Poor. Robin Hood would take a penny from her every time she was captured. She kept a special coin purse just for those pennies.

A hundred other little things about Christopher steam-rolled through her mind. And soon he would be growing up and leaving her. You're over-reacting, she told herself angrily. You'll be able to handle it tomorrow.

She took the Valium finally. Julie was coming for her at 9.00, to collect her for that doctor's appointment.

Theresa woke at six, from a childishly happy dream in

which she and Christopher were on a space shuttle going to the moon. It was just the two of them in the capsule, and they were playing some kind of space draughts. She awakened with sickened disappointment to find herself earthbound and alone.

Then she remembered Julie. And the anxiety turned to an odd kind of terror – the kind she hadn't had in years.

I can't go with her to the doctor, Theresa thought. I'll tell her I've changed my mind. It would be impossible, almost obscene, walking by Julie's side, letting people think they were friends.

But it would be interesting to see how she handles being told she's going to die, a clear cheerful voice said suddenly in Theresa's mind. She clapped her hands over her mouth as if she had spoken aloud. Sick, shameful thought. Oh, God. What sort of woman am I?

And of course Julie was not going to be told she was going to die.

Theresa dressed and sat on the bed waiting. She made herself think of the daycare centre in Tucson that was scheduled to open that month – her first fully-fledged daycare centre for handicapped children. She thought about it until nine a.m. when Julie knocked slowly and softly on the door and Theresa rose to let her in. Julie stood there tentatively – just as she had stood on Theresa's doorstep a million years ago.

'No,' Michael said. 'It's out of the question.'

'I want to invite Julie for a visit,' Terry kept repeating. 'I've been worrying all day about what Eunice told me in the toystore. Julie needs help. I think I can give it to her.'

'You?' Michael sneered. 'What can you do? Julie hasn't been in your life for years. She doesn't even care about you – don't you remember? She didn't give us a wedding present.'

'I remember,' Terry told him coldly. 'And if I choose to forget it, so should you. What's Julie to you? Nothing. But she means a hell of a lot to me.'

Afraid that she had been too domineering – never a good idea if she wanted to get her way – she tried a more yielding approach. 'I know you don't like company, Michael,' she said, 'but I'll see Julie's completely out of your way, I promise. And,' she added lightly, but a slight skim of bitterness rose to the top of the remark, 'if you keep on with these crazy office hours, you probably won't see her *or* me for weeks on end anyway.'

'Weeks?' he yelped. 'No way, Terry. No way. She can stay one week, and after that it's goodbye.'

'All right,' Terry said eagerly. 'One week.' She snuggled happily against him, but he did not respond. She wondered why, exactly, he was so upset. Was it because she had not been feminine enough in her urging? Was it because she had got her way? Or was it simply because he was jealous of her friendship with Julie?

'Eunice makes her sound as if she's changed a great deal,' she told Michael encouragingly.

He said nothing.

They saw each other at the same moment – Julie, wearing an Indian cotton dress, her hair loose and wild, getting off the plane. Terry, anxious-looking, afraid she was waiting for the wrong flight. When they saw each other, they both began to laugh.

They walked towards the baggage claim, still laughing. Months, years, disappeared, became unreal, were absorbed into nothingness like the steps of the escalator they were descending.

At the bottom, Terry took Julie's travelling bag from

her shoulder. 'That's too heavy for you,' she scolded.

'You said that about my lunchbox.'

'The first day of first grade.'

'Nothing has changed.'

But when they were waiting for the luggage and Terry could look at Julie less excitedly, she could see how great the change had really been. There was a new boldness about Julie – in her stance, in her look, in the things she was saying. It was the boldness of one who has done everything.

Terry felt sad. She thought wryly about how hard Julie's mother had always tried to keep her from the real world. '*Today is my little girl's fifth birthday* . . .' But in the end, people always broke away and did exactly what they had to do, what they were meant to do.

The drive to Terry's house seemed to take a long time. The two women didn't speak much, and the silences were difficult. Finally they arrived. Terry parked the car in the driveway, and, taking Julie's bags, started up the path to the front door. She had her key in the lock before she realized that Julie was not behind her. Julie was still standing by the car, holding on to the door handle with both hands. As though it were a life preserver, Terry thought.

'Well, here we are.' Terry talked rapidly, pretending she hadn't seen Julie's white knuckles fiercely clutching the handle. 'Come on in! Michael probably won't be here yet. He really works so hard – it's terrible. I keep telling him he should let his assistant take on some of the drudgery. Hurry up, Julie – I can't wait for you to see Christopher!'

It was only then that Julie let go of the car door and came up the front path.

It was nine-thirty that evening. Dinner was long over. Michael was not home yet and Christopher was in his room, the little night-light shining under the door. Terry and Julie were sitting in the den. The room was over-stuffed with furniture, the sofas covered in perhaps too bright a

177

fabric, but there was a certain lazy comfort in it all.

The two women listened peacefully to the sweet songs on the radio, and drank a bottle of a dull white wine that an acquaintance of Michael's had given him for Christmas. Julie had asked for Cinzano, but Terry, who had never even heard of it, looked wildly through the drinks cupboard, then announced with disgust that they were out of it.

Julie lay on the sofa doing nothing, glancing with a half-smile at the earnest rows of 'Great Books' lining the wall. Terry started the week's mending.

'You're very lucky, Terry,' Julie said suddenly, so lightly that Terry thought she was kidding.

'Sure. If you call doing four loads of washing a week, and baking brownies for the Cub Scouts every Saturday lucky!' she bantered back.

'But you love it, don't you?'

Terry was silent a moment. 'I guess I do,' she admitted. 'I know it's not fashionable, but I do.' And then Michael's voice, telling her how narrow she was becoming, rose unbidden to her mind.

'It's funny,' Julie said thoughtfully. 'I guess anyone who knew us as children would have guessed it would have ended up the opposite way. You were always the ambitious one, the dreamer, the one with plans. And I was the good little girl who just wanted to stay home with Mummy. And the way things turned out – well, you're the lucky one, Terry,' she said again.

Terry looked over at Julie's enigmatic face. Yes, she supposed she was. At least she was safe and knew where she was going. But tonight, hearing Julie make the comparison of their two lives, it occurred to Terry that maybe that wasn't the whole story. That maybe it was her own life that was lacking. That it was unnaturally safe, tame, drugged, like a dog in a pet shop. You're getting narrow. Michael's words invaded her mind again. Terry felt anxious; foolishly anxious, she told herself; as if something devastating was being unleashed tonight. But she had no idea what it was.

She looked over at her friend again, wondering a little wistfully what experiences Julie had had through the years, what lessons she had been taught. Terry knew they were lessons and experiences she herself could never understand or catch up with. Her friend had grown, and she had not.

Oh, well, she sighed. Oh, what the hell. And she sighed again and did the few final stabbing stitches on Christopher's blue jean patch.

'How is your mother, Julie?' she asked at last.

Julie shrugged. 'Didn't Eunice tell you? I had to put her in the Motion Picture Home. It was the best thing – she was just getting worse and worse.' Then she laughed shortly. 'Mummy has the distinction of being the youngest, prettiest, and nuttiest patient they've ever had.' Abruptly she lit a cigarette. It was the first time Terry had ever seen Julie smoke.

'And what about your dad?' Julie asked, exhaling.

'Oh, he's fine,' Terry smiled. 'He's planning on going back to college. After all these years.'

Julie didn't smile back, and Terry was aware of how desperately dull all this must seem to her. But, 'I remember your parents very well,' Julie said quietly. 'I cried for a long time when I read in the paper that your mother had died. I still think about her a lot. I remember her teaching me how to swim one summer. I kept wishing she was my mother. She was so – so easy.'

Terry was stunned. 'But you and your mother were so close,' she stammered.

'Were we?' Julie smiled. 'Yes. I guess we were. At least, as long as I did exactly what she wanted me to.' Her voice was very light and cool, and the smile stayed. 'Mummy almost died giving birth to me. Sometimes I wish she had. It would have made things so much easier.'

Terry was shocked.

'I never had much of a childhood, you know,' Julie went

on. 'Mummy saw to that. The closest I came to having one were those weekends I spent at your house – climbing trees, going to the beach, teasing that ridiculous brother of yours.' Abruptly, she changed the subject. 'And what about you?' she asked. 'Are you a good mother?'

Terry felt a stab of depression. 'Christopher's the most important thing in the world to me,' she said humbly, 'but I end up fussing at him all the time. Michael tries less hard, and Christopher loves him more.' She put down the mending, appalled. She couldn't believe she had admitted such a thing.

'Oh, come on; I'm sure you're a wonderful mother,' Julie said. 'You always were. To me, at any rate,' she added lightly.

'Ah, but you grew up, didn't you?' Terry gave a forced laugh, surprised that it still hurt. 'And so will Christopher.'

'Do you ever think about what you'll do then?' Julie asked.

'I sometimes think about going back to school. Like father, like daughter, right? I like this daycare thing I've started. Maybe I'll try to do something with that.'

'Yes.' Julie nodded, as if this pleased her. 'That would suit you.'

'And what about you, Julie?' Terry trod the new ground hesitantly. 'What are your plans?'

A very odd look, almost one of fear, came over Julie's face. Then as quickly as it had come, it was gone. 'Washing my face and going to bed,' she said. And she rose to her feet and kissed Terry goodnight.

Julie woke up in the unfamiliar room. For a moment she felt afraid. Then the clean, scentless flowered sheets around her and the suburban streetlamp outside her window quietened her. She was in Terry's guest bedroom. But what had awakened her? The noise came again. It was Christopher, in the room next to hers. He was crying.

Julie sat up in bed, hesitating. She guessed she should wake Terry. But the thought of tending Christopher herself rose and stayed with her.

Swiftly she came into the nursery. Christopher lay sobbing in a wet knot of fear.

'Wake up,' she whispered. He opened his eyes. She sat on the bed. 'What's the matter, baby?'

'I'm not a baby,' he whispered.

'I know that,' she reassured him, 'but I call all the men I know 'baby'. I guess that keeps me from being so afraid of you big guys.'

Christopher was appeased. They sat together in the darkness.

'Did you have a bad dream?'

'It was the alligator dream.'

She did not need to hear more. 'That can be a bad one,' she said, and then she asked suddenly, 'Did your mommy tell you anything about me before I came?'

'No.'

'Oh,' Julie said, flatly.

'Wait a minute,' Christopher said, watching her with huge night-light-lit eyes. 'I guess Mom did tell me about you. She said that when she was as old as me, you were her best friend like I've got Artie.'

'That's right,' Julie told him, smiling. 'Absolutely right. Tell me about Artie.'

'He's okay,' Christopher shrugged. 'But we fight a lot.'

Julie laughed. 'So did your mother and I. You think you and Artie will be best friends all your life?'

'Oh, no,' Christopher shook his head. 'Mom won't let us. She says it's the worst mistake you can make to have just one friend.'

'She said that, did she?' Julie asked quietly.

Christopher slipped back beneath the blankets. 'You look a lot younger than Mom,' he said critically. 'And you smell a lot younger, too.'

Julie considered him. 'One day this week, let's go to the park,' she said. Then she added casually, 'Would you like to go with your Mom, too, or should it just be the two of us?'

'Just the two of us,' he said, without hesitation.

Julie gave a slight smile. Then she kissed him on his damp, busy brow, and went back to her room.

The next morning Terry let Julie sleep late, and woke her by bringing in a tray full of oatmeal and brown sugar. Then she sat on Julie's bed. They didn't talk much, but it was pleasant. Michael had already left for work, and Christopher for school.

And then the two women got dressed and Terry showed Julie around town. At first Terry was very self-conscious. She apologized for the drabness of the little Main Street, and she tried to show it off at its best by pointing out the glamorous new department store at the far end.

But Julie seemed genuinely interested in the real town – the dinky five and dime, the art deco drugstore. Before long, Terry relaxed and the two of them flowed into the kind of day that they had had together in olden times. They tried on ridiculous clothes, killed themselves laughing at how they looked in rainbow coloured wigs, and even had ice-cream sodas.

Julie was a wonderful guest. Everything amused her, interested her, and there was nothing about Terry's life she did not want to hear about. She laughed at Terry's stories about the parents at the daycare centre. She sympathized about the sprinkler system. And she applauded Terry's plans for the new green guest bathroom.

They ended up at the new department store after all. Julie went immediately to the bathroom shop and bought a beautiful green and white limoges cup and soap dish. It amazed Terry to see her writing a cheque so large for objects so small.

When the wrapped packages were given to Julie, she

handed them to Terry with a smile. 'For your new guest bathroom,' she said. Then, as Terry opened her mouth to protest, 'It's your wedding present,' Julie said. 'I never gave you one.'

Terry stood still and let the warm waves of pleasure lap her from all sides.

At the end of that wonderful day, it was good to drive home in Terry's jingling old station wagon that still smelled from a two-year-old orange juice spill. It was good to pull into the driveway, watching the sunset splash its light on to the tulip beds. Good to get out of the car, laden with parcels. And good to be sitting in the den once more.

Terry was knitting a vest for Michael's birthday present. She was counting the stitches, listening to the sounds of Christopher playing in his room, thinking that life was a continuum, and what a fortunate woman she was to have such a child, and such a good friend come back into her life.

Julie sat very still. She drank a glass of vodka, and did not speak until it was finished. 'It was a lovely day,' she said finally.

'I'm glad,' Terry smiled. 'Plenty more where today came from.'

Julie, as she rested her head against the brightly-flowered couch, was pale – so pale that her make-up stood out from her skin like a garish clown's mask. Terry was saddened to see the web of cosmetics and creams put on with such infinite subtlety betraying Julie in this way.

'I keep thinking,' Julie said, 'of what a nice life you have.' Her smile, twisted out of shape, made the made-up mask look even more startling. 'I'm so lonely,' she said quietly.

Terry was horrified, embarrassed, scared of pressing too close. 'Don't be lonely,' she jerked out finally, in a helpless Pollyanna voice. 'You always have me, you know.'

Again, Julie smiled. 'No,' she said, 'I don't. Though I used to think I did. For all those years, I had you and Mummy both to keep me from the real world. You two would take care of me always and keep me safe.' She paused and drank more vodka. Her throat was so transparent that Terry fancied she could see the liquid flowing down. 'But the night Mummy took the pills I saw that no one can keep you safe. And you,' Julie shrugged. 'You promised me that night that you'd always be there for me. Then you came to me a week later and said you were getting married and moving to Chicago. You didn't even have the decency to look sorry.'

She raised her head. Terry was unnerved by the look in her eyes. 'Oh, Julie,' she began numbly, but the words lay on her lips and died. There was nothing she could say.

'Well, we all have to grow up some time, don't we?' Julie straightened up on a low, brittle laugh. 'And grow up I certainly did. There are a whole lot of people who can tell you about the things I've done since I've grown up. I was in jail once,' she said casually. 'Did Eunice tell you? In Mexico. For drugs. A boyfriend and me. I remember lying in the cell, and just picturing your face and Mummy's face. Isn't that funny?'

'Oh, Julie, please,' Terry said unsteadily.

Julie looked over at her. 'But that's all over now,' she said gently. She stretched her arms high over her head. 'I don't have to prove anything to anyone anymore. Now I just want to rest and let it all go by. I'm living in Mummy and Daddy's old house in Palm Springs these days. It's nice. All the old furniture's still there, and the books. I even found some school papers in my room – I sit at the desk sometimes and look at them. But I don't sleep in my room. I sleep in Mummy's bed. The linen cupboard's still full of the sheets she used to use. I keep thinking that one night I'm going to wake up and there they'll both be, Mummy and Daddy, home from a party, bringing me a napkin full of petits fours. Just like they used to.'

Terry was aghast at the thought of Julie sleeping in that bed of ghosts. It seemed so symbolic and unreal, like the

184

awful ending to some characters in an Ibsen play. But the small hand before the pale face was no fictitious character's hand – it was Julie's. And that was Julie's voice telling her these gruesome things, and that was Julie's hair spilling over onto the flowered couch.

And suddenly Terry was once again the five year old who had told the first grade class that the metal monstrosity was her own lunchbox. Because Julie needed protecting.

She put down the knitting, and scowled in the old bossy Terry way. 'What sort of morbid nonsense is that?' she demanded. 'It's sheer foolishness, staying in your parents' house – it would be enough to drive anyone crazy! Forget the whole plan, Julie, and listen to me,' she rapped out. 'What you need is a nice cheerful place, with bright young people around you.' She paused. 'Julie!' Her eyes and smile popped open wide. 'Move near us!'

Without waiting for Julie's reaction, Terry went right on. She could really feel the old take-charge muscle flex and stretch. 'I think it would be utterly ideal!' she cried. 'I could find you an apartment while you pack up the Palm Springs house, and maybe even a job. Michael has a friend whose receptionist just left to get married, and he's looking for someone new. You'd be just wonderful at it – and it would be a good start for you. You'd meet all sorts of people, and – ' she slapped the chair in sudden excited realization – 'and Julie! I think I've even got a man lined up for you!'

There was a pause. The two women looked at each other, and then they both began to laugh hysterically.

'Well,' Julie told Terry, with a last wipe at her eyes, 'I guess you're still the best person to run my life after all.' Then she came over and put her thin, delicately scented arms around Terry's neck. 'No, Terry,' she said quietly. 'But oh, you're such a little sweetheart.'

Terry smiled shakily, ashamed and deflated because she was evidently not to be taken seriously anymore. Suddenly she felt very tired, and she wanted the whole conversation to end. 'It's nearly seven,' she said. 'Michael said he'd be on time tonight, and I haven't even started dinner yet.'

'You've been entertaining me all day,' Julie said. 'You shouldn't have to cook. Why don't I treat us to some take-away food?'

'Oh, Michael wouldn't like that,' Terry told her. Then, catching Julie's expression, she added quickly, 'Anyway, I like to cook.'

'I never would have believed that of you,' Julie said, smiling.

Terry stood up. 'Well, it's true,' she answered, too quickly.

She went into the kitchen. Julie came to the door and watched for a moment, but did not offer to help. Soon she walked back to the den. Turning towards the spice cabinet to get the sage, Terry could see her friend's reflection in the dining-room mirror.

Julie was brushing, smoothly and methodically, her stunning wiry hair. Something made a connection in Terry's mind, but she could not think what it was. It kept teasing her until, putting the casserole in the oven, she remembered. The Plaza Hotel when she was fifteen. The 'Tennessee Waltz'. The two boys in leather jackets, forbidden by Terry to come up to the room. And Julie waiting for them, brushing, brushing out her hair.

Michael came home on time, as promised. Terry opened the front door.

'Hi, Terry,' he said. 'How was your day?'

Then Julie stepped out of the shadows. Michael looked at her for a moment. 'Hello, Julie,' he said flatly. He did not kiss her, or even shake her hand.

Then the timer went off in the kitchen, and Terry excused herself. She told Julie and Michael to go into the den and relax while she served up the dinner.

As Terry took out the best flowered serving dishes from

the cabinets, she listened. She could hear David Brinkley on the television, but no other sounds. Her heart began to beat rapidly, nervously. It wasn't going well out there in the den – she could tell it wasn't going well. Damn Michael, she thought in exasperation. He expected her to be charming to all his stupid clients, night after night – and yet he couldn't even be bothered to make conversation with her best friend. Terry felt miserably angry at him for spoiling her daydream of the happy visit. She burned her hand taking the casserole out of the oven.

'Dinner!' she called at last, forcing herself to speak gaily.

Michael and Julie came into the room. They sat down and Michael said grace. And as she sat there with eyes diligently closed, Terry had the most curious feeling. She felt that Michael's and Julie's eyes were not closed. That they remained open.

When grace ended, Terry looked quickly around. Julie was smiling at her. 'This casserole does smell heavenly,' she said.

There was not much conversation during dinner, and what there was was leaden. Terry was sorry that she had sent Christopher off to spend the night at Artie's house. His endless chirps and chatter would have filled so many of the holes.

She grew madder and madder at Michael. Surely he could *try*, she thought. Even if he hates Julie, he owes it to me to try.

Lying in bed that night, Terry couldn't sleep. The pillows and sheets protested under her every time she moved. The room was damp from the dripping rain.

'Michael?' she said in a low voice.

'What?' he stirred.

'Why do you hate Julie?' she asked in a low voice.

'Jesus Christ, Terry,' Michael moaned. 'Give me a break. It's two o'clock in the morning, and you woke me up to ask me that?'

But Terry knew he hadn't been asleep.

It was Wednesday, the August sky still overcast with muggy clouds. Terry and Julie were driving home from grocery shopping. Terry's face was tired, unpretty, as she sighed in the dismal heat. Julie, sitting beside her, watched block after block of upstanding, self-centred little suburban houses go by.

'I'll tell you something I bet you didn't know,' she broke the silence finally in a light voice. 'I knew Michael before you did.'

Terry stared stupidly before her. She paused to let a little boy run across the road. 'What?' she asked at last.

Julie lit a cigarette, studying Terry's blank face sidelong. 'That's right. I knew his sister Jamie. We took ballet together. Michael came to pick her up one day, and that was how we met. A few months before you two did.'

Terry's face grew more strained, more colourless, as she tried to take it in. Ballet class. Fat little girls with tutus. Julie. And yet something so black, so foreboding was settling in front of her eyes. 'Are you saying you dated Michael?' she asked in a careful voice.

'He had a red Volkswagen,' Julie said.

Terry experienced a curious sensation – one she got during a fever – that her hands were swelling up before her, swelling into balloons. Soon I won't be able to keep the car on the road. Julie and Michael. Julie had known Michael. But why, why had they never told her?

At last Terry reached her own driveway and pulled shakily into it. Christopher was playing with his plastic football on the front lawn. High up into the air he threw it. Each time it spun in an erratic elliptical curve, then fell with a dead sound into the grass. He did not seem to mind that he was never able to catch it. He was shouting something to his mother as she pulled in. That there was a telegram on the hall table.

Terry opened the envelope a sliver at a time so that the bad news could not leap out all at once. But what she saw, after she read the words, were only wonderful pictures. Her father playing with the delicate little train set in the garage. Her father playing 'Heart and Soul' with her on the piano. Her father grinning with triumph as he wrote the cheque for his first semester's college tuition.

Julie came swiftly into the room. 'What is it?'

'My father's had a heart attack. I've got to go to California.' Terry groped for the telegram again. 'Yes,' she repeated unsteadily. 'I've got to go.' Then helplessly she put her hands before her eyes. 'How can I?' she demanded, whimpering. 'How on earth can I? Who's going to look after Christopher? Who's going to look after Michael?'

Julie was watching her. 'You'll go,' she said calmly. 'Because I'll be here. I'll look after everything.' Then she added, oddly, 'We owe it to each other.'

Terry, overcome, wept. And behind her, she could hear Christopher's glad shout. 'Oh, boy! Aunt Julie's staying! Aunt Julie's staying!'

Julie held her. It was astonishing how strongly those delicate arms could hold.

'Julie,' Michael said.

It was after dinner on their second evening alone together. Once again, she had fixed him scrambled eggs and toast. He was drinking. It was his fifth vodka since dinner. And because she was nervous, she had gone into the bathroom and taken one of the small white pills hidden in her make-up case.

'No,' she answered.

They were in the den, watching the news. Julie was in the armchair, her delicacy enfolded and overborne by its chintz. He was sitting on the edge of the sofa. He stood and moved to her, putting his own arms on the arms of the chair, in such a way that she was pinned there – as a child might do in a game.

Christopher was asleep in his room, the glow from the night light beating loyally under the door.

'Yes,' Michael said. 'Julie, yes.' He bent his head on to her breast and whispered, 'Having you here – it's like a dream. All those years. And now you're here.'

'And Terry's gone,' Julie said drily.

He jerked up. 'You've seen us together,' he said angrily. 'Can't you tell? There's nothing there.'

'Only Christopher,' she said. 'And the fact that she loves you.'

'No,' he said, without lowering his eyes. 'She hasn't loved me for a long time.' He was still leaning over her. Julie could smell his breath on her face. It smelled of real life.

'Julie,' he said in a low quick voice. 'You're lovelier than you were before. In high school, you were like a goddess to me. I was so afraid to see you again – I was so afraid that you had changed – that you had lost your magic. But everything's the same.'

'It's not the same!' Julie cried.

'No. It's not the same,' Michael whispered. 'I feel like an old man these days – can you imagine how you must look to me now?'

Julie tossed back her hair involuntarily. For a second she felt the exhilaration of that girl sitting on the school gatepost on a windy day, meeting a boy in a red Volkswagen. 'Michael,' she said gently. 'You don't love me. You may have when we were sixteen, but you don't now. And I'm not here to see you. I'm here to see Terry. We've been friends for a long, long time.'

Michael shook his head. 'Julie, that childhood friendship hasn't mattered to her in years. The only reason she invited you here was out of pity. She told me so.'

The colour swam into Julie's cheeks in a hot, stinging flood. Michael was pressing closer to her. He was kissing the long tendrils of hair now. At first she hardly noticed –

what he had just said was eating like acid through her mind. Go to hell, Terry, she thought.

Michael was kissing her neck now, her cheeks. 'But what I feel for you isn't pity,' he was whispering hoarsely. He kissed her lips, over and over, and murmured against them, 'I need you. Oh, God, Julie. I need you.'

His lips were warm and wanting. She heard a woman moaning and realized only gradually that it was herself. She had always loved his kisses. The pill she had taken began to build its dream world in her head. She was in the red Volkswagen, being kissed by a boy. He was so strong; clean-cut. And he loved her more than any boy ever had. 'You're a goddess,' he kept saying. 'Marry me. Marry me.'

She frowned. Some other Julie, in some other life, had actually told this god to go away. Crazy Julie. Bad bad things had happened to her because she had said no to him. She had had men who were cruel, and her Mummy went mad and she ended up alone and afraid. But it would have all been different, it would have been a sweet sane life if she had said yes to this boy with his deep, wild kisses.

But she must remember – she was not that other Julie; she was cleverer than that; she was not going to make the same mistake.

'Stay with me; stay with me,' he kept murmuring. 'Let me take care of you.'

Take care of you. The little Julie-boat was cuddled in the harbour, in the waiting arms. They were so warm and nice, those arms, but they kept changing. They were Mummy's arms. Then they were Terry's arms. The Count's arms. Daddy's arms. Michael's arms. Michael's arms.

'My haven,' she whispered, and pulled him down to her.

Terry returned from California on a Monday. The afternoon was grave and beautiful. From the windows of the straining plane, the fields and farmhouses of Illinois looked simple and good.

California was no longer home to her in any sense now. Terry even made herself whisper it. This land beneath her was her only home.

Her DC-10 arrived at O'Hare. Meticulously, Terry checked the floor and seat pockets to make sure nothing had been left behind. Nothing had.

The airport was crowded, with parents saying goodbye to their children going off to school. Each weeping mother, each damp hug, each cry of 'Call us when you get there!' brought a separate shrill pain to Terry's throat. Anguish, anguish, parents and children having to say goodbye. She craved only to be home now, with her own baby, craved Christopher's fat little arms plunged around her neck.

She found a taxi at last, and chattered so nervously that the driver asked if this was her first visit to Chicago. At last they pulled in front of the house. How serene and sturdy it looked, her home. Her home! Terry caught a glimpse of Christopher in the back yard, playing with his football. But she made herself wait – denied herself that greeting until she had paid the driver and pulled the bags from the car.

And then, free, waving the Disneyland pennant she had brought back for him, she ran around the side of the house, panting with joy. 'Christopher!' she cried.

He gazed at the pennant wordlessly, and she kissed, over and over, the soft feathers of blond hair on his neck. But he seemed strangely stiff.

'I missed you so much,' she said over and over. 'Did you miss me?' But he said nothing. 'Was everything all right while I was gone?' Terry asked, a sudden fear at her heart.

'I guess so.'

'Did Auntie Julie take good care of you?'

'I guess so.'

Terry smiled again. 'Well, then if everything's OK, how come I don't get a hello kiss?'

Christopher shook his head firmly. 'Daddy told me men

don't kiss,' he announced. 'Men shake hands.' He held out his small hand to her.

Terry tried to keep from bursting into tears. 'Well, now, that's not always true, you know,' she told him reasonably. 'Look at Daddy. Daddy kisses people. He kisses you, dosn't he? And me?'

'Daddy kisses Aunt Julie,' the little boy answered.

The pennant fluttered to the ground.

'You bitch! You traitor! How could you?' Terry seized the thin arm. She wanted to bite through it with her fingers, snap the twigs that were Julie's bones.

But Julie pulled away with a wild strength. Terry slapped her as hard as she could. A white ghost hand remained on Julie's whiter face.

'To do this to me – after I invited you here – out of friendship –'

'Out of pity!' Julie cried. 'Oh, I know all about it. Michael told me. Poor old Julie with her awful life – let's see if we can't give her a crumb or two of happiness. Well, who do you think made my life so awful, Terry? It was you.'

'You're crazy!' Terry blazed. 'I haven't even thought about you in years!'

'Yes; that's just the point, isn't it?' Julie cried. 'For so many years you made me dependent on you. And then, just when I needed you most, you discarded me. Just like that.'

'You're twisting everything,' Terry cried.

'Really?' Julie asked quietly. 'All I know is that I've spent most of the last seven years in hell, making mistake after mistake, just trying to start out as a person again, since I couldn't be Terry's little shadow anymore. And all the time it turns out that you've never even given me a thought. So consider this my little revenge.'

'My God,' Terry choked. 'I hate you. Get out of here! I never want to see you again. You're a monster – a monster!'

Julie considered this. 'Not really,' she said with a sad smile. 'Just a victim. And now you're one, too.'

Terry picked up the toaster and hurled it at Julie's head. Julie ducked, and as she reached the door, she turned around. 'But do you know what the funny part of all this is?' And there were tears suddenly flooding her face. 'You mean a thousand times more to me than any man ever could, and yet I'm leaving for California with Michael this afternoon. I'm not even sure why. And that's the really funny part.'

Michael came out of the bedroom and paused by the kitchen table where she was sitting. He had with him the large plaid Samsonite suitcase they had bought so hopefully for a trip to Greece that now would never happen.

'Goodbye, Terry,' he said.

Motionless at the table, she pretended not to hear. In some crazy way she thought that if she did not answer his goodbye, he could not go. But Michael was not bound by this wishful rule.

He reached the door. 'I never wanted all this to come out,' he said. 'But in the long run it's better for us both.'

Better, she thought. What a curious way of saying that my life is over.

There had been a day in fall when she was very young. When she had crawled into the bushes on Michael's front lawn and watched him. Watched his arms so firm and brown, his crisp curling hair, and she felt her heart rise and sink, rise and sink, with a terrible, painful, unending love.

Michael closed the front door behind him. And it was over.

CHAPTER SIX

At ten-forty, Theresa was sitting in the waiting room of Dr Richard Shapiro, PD, OB, GYN. The office was horribly cheery, with comic needlepoint 'doctor' plaques, last year's Christmas cards on the mantel, children's drawings behind lucite frames. Two women in the waiting room were pregnant. They flipped smilingly through baby magazines. But the faces of the other patients were blighted. And the old man waiting for his wife was bent over, holding his fragile head in fragile hands. Theresa was frightened sitting there – as if just being in the office was making her vulnerable to these other people's dooms.

She looked at her watch. It was ten-forty-five. Julie had gone in at nine-twenty. But of course, Theresa reminded herself, the doctor never comes into the examining room right away. They make you wait forever. She had a flashed thought of Julie waiting on the table, the way she had when she had gone to the doctor as a child, her feet dangling down, icy, icy.

Then from somewhere on the other side of the closed door there came a low, suffering groan. It echoed on and on. Theresa stiffened. Was that Julie? She had never heard Julie groaning. She wouldn't recognize the sound.

She made herself relax back into the green leather chair. Her mind was full of dizzying eddies. She did not know what she ought to be feeling. She wished somebody could tell her. Pity, sorrow, triumph, terror – all these things paraded silently down the ramp of her mind. Mostly, everything felt unreal. What was she doing in the office of Dr Richard Shapiro, PD, OB, GYN? Waiting for Julie. Just like that. Julie, whom she had thrown from her house seven years before, forever.

The groan came again, louder and more sharp. Theresa knew now it wasn't Julie; because, when he heard the sound, the old man in the chair opposite hers flung down his hands with an answering moan and hurried, scuttling like a shaking crab, to the inter-office door. His frantic efforts to rush in were stopped with pitiful ease by a young blonde nurse. The old man was led back to his chair.

Theresa kept her eyes fixedly away from his face. If I don't look at him, she thought, then maybe it won't happen to me – or to Julie.

On the table beside Theresa was an issue of 'Highlights Magazine for Children'. She had a sudden vivid memory of herself as an eight year old, sitting in the hospital waiting room, engrossed in a copy of 'Highlights', trying to find the '10 Hidden Objects'. She had just found the squirrel in the sky when the doctor came over to say that her grandmother had died.

The eddies in her mind were worse. Theresa pulled the copy of 'Highlights' on to her lap. The magazine felt very heavy. She had trouble turning the pages. She found the Hidden Objects page and began to search through it with fingers that buckled and shook.

The inner door of the doctor's office opened, and Julie came out. A nurse took her arm in the glass anteroom and spoke to her. Theresa could see the lips moving soundlessly, with lives of their own. It was as if the glass antechamber were the two sheets of glass that bright, dead butterflies are pressed between.

When Julie came out, Theresa was still holding the 'Highlights Magazine for Children'. She had not been able to find a single one of the Hidden Objects.

Julie looked at her with a faint smile. They left the office. 'What did the doctor say?'

Julie shrugged. 'Not much. I have to go in for more tests.'

'But did he say there – was a problem?'

A pause. When Julie answered, her voice was steady. 'He doesn't think there is.'

'I'm glad,' Theresa said carefully. But she had always known when Julie was lying. 'You want to have lunch somewhere?' she asked in a low voice.

'At the Palm Court,' Julie said. 'I'd like for us to go there again.'

They began to walk slowly down Fifth Avenue along the Park.

'Is there anybody you want me to call?'

'No, Terry. But I'm glad you came with me.'

The day was full of flirting white clouds – a cottage cheese sky, Mrs Garvey used to call it.

'Do you remember Binky Elliot?' Julie asked suddenly. 'That little girl who died of a brain tumour? On the day of her funeral, you told me that I was going to live to be very old.'

'Did I?'

'Yes.' Julie smiled wryly. 'And I thought you were always the honest one of us two.'

They walked along in silence. The wind was gentle and sad. A battered school bus filled with children coming from an excursion to the Met came roaring down the Avenue. The children stuck their heads out the windows, screaming with freedom and self-importance.

Julie smiled. 'Remember?' she asked.

Theresa frowned. She said distinctly, 'I'm afraid I've forgotten nearly everything about those days.'

'I guess you have more important things to think about.'

'Something like that.'

'Well, I remember it all,' Julie said. 'And we had plenty of good times on the school bus. Don't you remember the little girl you beat up just because she dared talk to me?'

197

Theresa could not bear to say she did.

'And when you got into trouble for it, I told the principal I had napped through the whole thing. I always was a rat,' Julie smiled. She looked at Theresa sidelong. 'But it was hard not to be, really. Because you always expected more than I could give.'

They walked another block in silence.

'I guess you must hate me very much.'

A great weariness fogged in front of Theresa's eyes. 'I don't know, Julie,' she said. 'What happened doesn't matter anymore. It was a long time ago. And I really think I've been much happier without Michael.'

'I'm glad,' Julie said earnestly. 'You deserve to be happy. You were always a very good person.'

Her words took Theresa by surprise. Am I? she wondered. Am I really? She was gripped by a sudden spasm of depression. She wished she were away from here, away from Julie, safely alone.

'I often wish,' Julie began, and her voice sounded as small as a child's, 'I often wish we might be friends again.'

'I don't think so,' Theresa said.

'But here we are – walking together like this,' Julie said, her voice trembling slightly. 'Did you ever think that would happen again?'

There was a pause.

'No.'

They were nearing the square in front of the hotel now. The breeze was growing fresher. The leaves bent and blew like the glorious standards of losing armies. In front of the fountain, a vendor was selling ice cream.

'When were you happiest in your life?' Julie asked suddenly.

Oh, God, if she would just shut up! But Theresa answered, 'I couldn't say.'

'I could.' Julie pointed to the vendor. 'It was one day when we went to the Park on Wilshire. We couldn't have

198

been more than seven. It was just an ordinary day, really. We got ice cream from a vendor who looked just like that one. Don't you remember? You always called him the man with the goldfish eyes. He said, 'Here comes the girl and her shadow again.' We kept asking which one of us was the girl and which one was the shadow, but he wouldn't say.

'We started running, and the wind was so strong it kept pushing us backwards. I don't know why – but I always look back on that moment as the happiest one in my life. Do you remember it?'

Of course Theresa remembered. The wind, the vendor, the girl and her shadow. 'We ate our ice creams in a secret place.' She almost whispered the words.

'In the cave behind the swings. You called it Narnia.'

'We both did.'

'Have you been happy these past years?' Julie asked her softly. Theresa did not answer. 'Things haven't turned out the way we thought they would when we were children, have they?' she went on.

'No. I guess they haven't.'

'They don't for most people.'

'No.'

'But life seems all right to them because they've forgotten what their dreams were like. But I will never, never forget.' Julie's eyes looked paler than Theresa had ever seen them. 'Those days when we were friends – I think it's all I want to remember of my life.' She smiled. 'Do you think that's terribly silly?'

Julie's words reverberated with profound sadness in Theresa's mind. How utterly pathetic, she thought, that all Julie has are those old memories. While I have so much. So much. The daycare centres. The awards. The speeches, Christopher. And they make me so happy – don't they? They're far better than any childhood dream ever was – aren't they? Aren't they? Oh, God.

She gave a rusty little smile. 'No,' she said. 'Maybe not so silly.'

'Oh, Terry,' Julie said, grasping her arm in a happy rush. 'Weren't those days the greatest! And what a crazy, wonderful team we were. Remember when we gave our watercolours the antique look?' She laughed. 'Remember your father and his train set? The time we caught Mrs Delaney on the Hill?'

'Spending the summers by your swimming pool,' Theresa murmured.

'Your eternal leg lifts.'

'Your eternal diets!'

'Hide and Seek.'

'Spying on your cook.'

'Spying on Timmy.'

'The Halloween you were Dorothy.'

'Your bat ears!'

The images came faster, faster. The two women were breathless now, flushed. They both began to laugh, as passers-by watched bleakly.

'Oh, thank you for remembering, Terry!' Julie cried. 'I couldn't bear it if you hadn't. All those things seem so much more real now, with both of us remembering.'

Theresa stopped walking. All the momentary euphoria was gone. She looked hard at the woman beside her. 'But I don't want them to become real again,' she said quietly. 'You forget, Julie. Those days are long past. Other days came after.'

Julie put a cold hand on her arm. 'Please forgive me, Terry,' she said. 'I never loved Michael. I don't know why I let it happen. I suppose I was jealous. Of so many things. You and Michael and Christopher. You not needing me anymore. Your life being so fulfilled when mine was so awful.'

'Julie,' Theresa said sharply. 'Let's not go on.'

'Yes,' Julie said firmly, her great eyes staring. 'Let's do

go on. I don't want there to be any misunderstandings between us – not anymore. Not now.' She took a deep breath. 'I hated you, Terry. That's the reason I took Michael away. As much as I loved you, I hated you too.' She twisted the strap of her leather handbag and spoke rapidly. 'From the time I was five years old, you did a terrible thing to me, Terry. You thought I was perfect. From the day I first met you, you tried to turn me into something I couldn't possibly be. I loved you so much, and I had to keep hiding what I really was. For fear you wouldn't love me anymore. And then – on that Choral Club trip to New York – something snapped. I couldn't pretend anymore. Remember that night I went off with those two boys? It was then that it happened. And you wouldn't forgive me. You said our friendship was over – that only a very immoral person could have done what I did.' She shook her head. 'You made me feel I was damned, Terry,' she said softly. 'That's a horrible feeling. So I started acting damned. I wasted so many years, doing all kinds of stupid things I didn't really want to do, just trying to prove – I don't even know what. Maybe that I was free.'

'I'm sorry,' Theresa said. 'I'm sorry if I did that to you.' Her voice was very low. 'How funny. I seem to have done it to everyone I've ever loved. I'm sorry,' she said again.

'Oh, forget it!' Julie cried, catching at her arm and shaking it. 'Listen to me, Terry,' she demanded. 'We've known each other for so many years, and there have been so many hurts on both sides. Do they really matter?' She laughed nervously. 'I'm really in no position to hold grudges any longer. I haven't got much time, Terry, and I can't afford to throw away those years that meant most to me. Please – please – couldn't we just cancel all those hurts out right now? One side against the other? I wish we could. And do you know what we'd be left with then? All our wonderful little memories. Just them. Pure and happy. For as long as we lived.'

Theresa paused. She looked down at the pale, tiny woman beside her. Tears of futility were incubating in her eyes. What Julie was asking was what a child might ask for. A fresh start. The past sponged clean. Just like that. And oh, wasn't it just like Julie to want what was completely impossible?

The tears were born.

'No, Julie,' she said gently. 'Don't you see? Far, far too much has happened.' But even as she spoke, she found herself reaching out and touching a strand of Julie's magical yellow hair.

The two women walked up the steps of the Plaza Hotel. In the large mirror, Julie caught sight of her hair messed by the wind, and she began to brush it smooth.

The great door rolled shut behind them.

Contemporary Women

Powerful, compelling novels about today's women . . .

Decisions   Freda Bright

The moment every working woman longs for . . . and every married woman dreads.

When Dasha returned to law school, her husband Jordan backed her all the way. And when she got a job with a top law firm, no one could have been more proud – until Dasha's career began outstripping his own. Now Dasha must make the most important decision of her life . . .

Friends of the Opposite Sex   Sara Davidson

'*A lively, intelligent novel remarkable for its thoughtful honesty*' EVENING STANDARD

Lucy is an independent woman with a flourishing career and plenty of love affairs. But she is thirty, and marriage and motherhood are suddenly appealing. Then she meets Joe, who wants both more and less than love – a working partnership – and Lucy must decide if they can ever be 'just good friends'.

The Rich and the Mighty   Vera Cowie

The news of billionaire Richard Tempest's death shakes the world's financial markets – and sends a tremor of anticipation through his rapacious stepchildren. But control of the Tempest fortune passes to a stranger. Elizabeth Sheridan, already a top model, has a cool head and a streak of ruthlessness. But are they enough to ensure her survival in the dangerous, decadent world of wealth to which she is suddenly heiress?

FONTANA PAPERBACKS

VIRGINIA ANDREWS
is a phenomenon

Flowers in the Attic

— the spellbinding story of the days four children spent imprisoned in the attic, days that stretched into years — just to gain their mother's inheritance . . .

Petals on the Wind

— continues the harrowing story of the children who escape their prison and are bent on revenge . . .

If There Be Thorns

— is the third novel in this extraordinary saga of the family who survive their loveless past and defied their black heritage . . .

Seeds of Yesterday

— completes the story of the Dollanganger family who return to the great house of their grandmother.

FONTANA PAPERBACKS

Romantic Suspense

Three outstanding romantic thrillers by great modern authors, in the marvellous storytelling tradition of Evelyn Anthony and Helen MacInnes.

In Safe Hands
Jane Sandford

Kate Harper was just a student but she was also the only child of the toughest Secretary of State for years. So she was kidnapped and held hostage for his resignation. Or that's what the kidnappers' leader, Irish doctor Conor, told her. Then, from the outside, new and unexpected dangers threatened her – and the kidnappers. Suddenly Kate was no longer safe – in anyone's hands.

The Servants of Twilight
Leigh Nichols

To his mother, Christine, Joey was an ordinary six-year-old boy. But to the Servants of Twilight he was an evil presence who must be destroyed. An encounter with a threatening old woman began a terrifying ordeal for Joey and Christine – a nightmare of horror that only the love of one man could enable Christine to survive.

Stillwatch
Mary Higgins Clark

Investigative journalist Pat Traymore was in Washington on a red-hot assignment – to find out about the Senator tipped to be the first woman Vice-President. But Pat had horrifying memories of the city, for something happened to her there as a child that scarred her life. Now her search for the sinister truth unleashes powerful and menacing forces against her . . .

FONTANA PAPERBACKS

New British Writers

Three rich, wonderful novels
by outstanding young British authors

A Splendid Defiance   Stella Riley

Justin Ambrose, a dashing and cynical Cavalier, was bored
with garrison life – until he fell in love with Abby, the sister
of a fanatic Roundhead rebel. With their hearts and
loyalties divided, and caught up in a passionate, forbidden
love affair, Abby and Justin watched the rival armies
prepare for a bloody confrontation.

The Skylark's Song   Audrey Howard

Zoe was born in the poorest street in Liverpool. As the
youngest of five children her life in the Merseyside slum
meant brutality, degradation and appalling poverty. But
Zoe was bright, sensitive and determined to escape.
Freedom would bring her wealth, luxury and love – and
heartache she could never have imagined . . .

A Season of Mists   Sarah Woodhouse

Ann Mathick had a dream. She wanted to make the run-
down Norfolk farm, which she had inherited from a
disreputable uncle, prosperous again. None of the county
believed she could do it. But the only man who could stop
Ann was Sir Harry Gerard, her dashing, reckless
neighbour – a very dangerous man to fall in love
with . . .

FONTANA PAPERBACKS

Fontana Paperbacks: Fiction

Fontana is a leading paperback publisher of both non-fiction, popular and academic, and fiction. Below are some recent fiction titles.

- [ ] THE ROSE STONE Teresa Crane £2.95
- [ ] THE DANCING MEN Duncan Kyle £2.50
- [ ] AN EXCESS OF LOVE Cathy Cash Spellman £3.50
- [ ] THE ANVIL CHORUS Shane Stevens £2.95
- [ ] A SONG TWICE OVER Brenda Jagger £3.50
- [ ] SHELL GAME Douglas Terman £2.95
- [ ] FAMILY TRUTHS Syrell Leahy £2.95
- [ ] ROUGH JUSTICE Jerry Oster £2.50
- [ ] ANOTHER DOOR OPENS Lee Mackenzie £2.25
- [ ] THE MONEY STONES Ian St James £2.95
- [ ] THE BAD AND THE BEAUTIFUL Vera Cowie £2.95
- [ ] RAMAGE'S CHALLENGE Dudley Pope £2.95
- [ ] THE ROAD TO UNDERFALL Mike Jefferies £2.95

You can buy Fontana paperbacks at your local bookshop or newsagent. Or you can order them from Fontana Paperbacks, Cash Sales Department, Box 29, Douglas, Isle of Man. Please send a cheque, postal or money order (not currency) worth the purchase price plus 22p per book for postage (maximum postage required is £3.00 for orders within the UK).

NAME (Block letters) _____

ADDRESS _____

_____

_____

While every effort is made to keep prices low, it is sometimes necessary to increase them at short notice. Fontana Paperbacks reserve the right to show new retail prices on covers which may differ from those previously advertised in the text or elsewhere.